T0380809

PAULI
THE GHOST

PAULI
THE GHOST

A Ground Zero Story of
Love and Terror

RESU ESPINOSA-FRINK

Archway Publishing books may be ordered through booksellers or by contacting:

Archway Publishing
1663 Liberty Drive
Bloomington, IN 47403
www.archwaypublishing.com
844-669-3957

Interior Graphics/Art Credit: Resu Espinosa-Frink

ISBN: 978-1-6657-6586-2 (sc)
ISBN: 978-1-6657-6587-9 (e)

Library of Congress Control Number: 2024919274

Print information available on the last page.

Archway Publishing rev. date: 01/28/2025

The dogmas of the quiet past are inadequate to the stormy present.
As our case is new, so, we must think anew, and act anew.
—Abraham Lincoln

To Pauli, who could teach us so much about love, if only he understood the duties of the heart

ONE

DIARY: NOTES FROM THE UNDERGROUND

I want to prepare a trap, but I find no one to volunteer to hold the bait while I activate the machinery. Some people have been very decent, and they didn't have to. Berta from Jehovah's Witnesses, for example, is not ready to bear testimony and communicate what she experienced, which would be essential to give this nightmare a shadow of validity by snatching with her declaration that irreverent mask called faked reality. But she still calls me at nine in the evening after her church meeting to see if I am well. She doesn't have to do this. But she feels better about herself for being this decent, even if it doesn't do me any good. It is like a life-and-death situation in the psychological dimension. One must risk one's own inner safety to save the other. Would I jump with someone I think I care for into his hell, that strange abyss? I do not find anyone who would go this far for me, although some people here and there talk about coming over to sleep one night in a spare room so the hate and strange events may disappear from my mind. They must add this "from your mind" silently to themselves, I feel it in the tone of their voices, the meaning of their stare.

After much plotting, I hit on a plan. Fred from Hungary, who knows something about terror and doors kicked open in the night and the swollen silence of disappearances, has invited me to sleep in his spare space one night. He says no. It is a failure-proof plan, but his memories of hard times return. It is impossible for him to do it, to exchange places with the persecuted and describe later to the police how one feels trapped in the power of the invisible presence. He backs down.

I can taste the panic through the text message he sends to say no. Everything disappears, swallowed up in the empty mouth of fear, including the ice cream trip planned, canceled in the name of some concern for the flu brought up earlier this week at a checkup event.

My plan is brilliant: he would come here after our walk—a regular event well-known to the neighbors—instead of me. We would wear dark-blue clothes and oversized hoodies because the fall is underway. It is quite cool. We are about the same size. The night and the intent to deceive easily erase any possible differences.

I would go someplace, not necessarily his apartment, which he may worry about, but a nearby motel or a coffee shop open until late. My car could stay in the driveway. Fred would enter the front door and go to the attic, turn on the lamplight, and read for a while, leaning on the futon's cushions. He'd maybe eat some fruit and go to the bathroom in the semi-dark, lighted by the cell phone, the way I do it. At the agreed time, he would turn off the light, as if to sleep. We would be in touch via texting. He would wait for the sound of the wireless waves hitting the window glass, the skylight panel. He would be alert to the arrival of the hands of fog and wire touching his body, climbing up his legs, grabbing the stomach, the belly, and the breasts. The voice, breathing hard, mumbling incomprehensible speech, would growl, blowing fetid air in Fred's nostrils, thinking they are mine.

He would say nothing and call the police or text me, saying he is a witness, and share the message with the police. Or he would wait for a future date to speak, but now he knows what it is like, how scary and disgusting.

But Fred says no. He doesn't want to make enemies. He wants nothing to do with the police. He is not interested in jumping into the nightmare with me, which would almost for sure be a redemption for his barren life, like in *Crime and Punishment*. And after the refusal, as it happens when one secretly knows to have failed, there is a growing distance, even sarcasm, laughing at how stupid this invisibility story sounds.

Your home is invaded with impunity. There is no privacy. You are spied on when exercising, typing, listening to music, showering, and sleeping. Your skin is examined. Your legs are tested by an electric wire as if they are fingerprints, certifying it is you. Your breathing is analyzed in the early morning, at night, and while speaking on the phone. And there is nothing you can do but move quickly to destroy whatever magnetic structure there is in his first try to set you up within a frame. Old Goat will try again, but your action is a temporary discouragement. Yes, he expects you to be quiet, passive, and submissive.

If you go to sleep, you abandon yourself to the hands of the Monster—It, the Old Goat—to his pleasure and rage. He cannot really touch you. He imagines he can, but he knows he can't. That enrages him even more. You have heard his growling as he slashed your blanket with his wireless fingers across your chest; you revealed his existence to the police. You will see now! Wait for his fury and his revenge. Watch out!

For the first time today, I am certain a microphone in my house is regularly managed by Soto Sr. It opened loudly when the homeless coordinator called me around two in the afternoon. And as his space became present in our line, a huge fart filled the line. Soto Sr., It, the Monster, turned off his parabolic microphone with trembling hands in a rush. Maybe the fart was an accident and not intended this time as the disrespecting tool that has become his signature.

I told the coordinator to text me to avoid having our conversations bombarded again. I have reported all this, and the police don't believe me. They could ask the coordinator, but that's too much trouble for this small thing, which I am probably imagining. They are sure I'm imagining.

After this, Soto Jr. played several of his Speedo-Hard tapes. They are about ten to fifteen seconds each, just a sudden, fast start of an engine at top speed, featuring a sustained muffler run. The longest, loudest one is thrown inside my attic room via a round-dancing wave of light as his car speeds by. Every Sunday morning.

Last night, Soto Sr. was here in my studio room the whole night, and the night before. He freezes my left arm, which emerges from his invisible iron plank, resembling a long flat tortilla dressed in my clothes but unrelated to my body, steps on my leg, blows into my nose. He tries to get cozy by stretching on my back. The punk!

I push him away, calling him disgusting, criminal, old, pusher, stinker, and abuser. I tell him I hope he's locked up in the darkest cell forever. He leaves for a little while. He comes back. He farts next to my mouth and leaves. I am sick to my stomach once more. I cross the living room, rushing to the bathroom. It smells of him, as if he had the capability of dumping awful smells here. I won't be able to turn off the light tonight. I must find a way to exorcise him.

Old Goat is in his fascist-general mood. I turn off the laptop where I've been typing this story, and in a frenzy of power unresolved, he tries to get under my blanket and bite at my thighs like a mouse that's been kept away from food. But he is tired, and I quickly escape to make my hiding place on the rug, covered by thick plastic. He can't find me. His stinking breath sounds out dissonances in the living room, coasting around the pianos like a drunkard blaspheming in a house of hungry children. His searching rod, the invisible bunch of photoelectric wires, distresses books and sheets of music. He is looking for me, growling, and breathing hard to show his impatience.

I hold my breath the best I can but open my eyes wide, although any such movement may attract his attention, through whatever it is that allows him to find me. With the rod, he lifts a corner of the plastic sheet under which I have slept since midnight, three hours at least, four maybe.

"Here she is," he murmurs darkly.

And the bodiless figure seems to straighten out, think, and disappear. I feel he has. I don't know. But I hang on to the idea that he's gone and then am able to smile.

Friday nights, Sundays, and the dark hours of snow season, with closing-downs and cancelations, have become special for the Sotos. With the forced extra time in the house, they have nothing to do but prepare meals and play with whatever new technological toy Junior brought for Father's entertainment: a cell phone without registration or identity, an unknown caller for hang-up calls, and a new round drone with geometrical designs to fly in my room when my light goes off, to be retrieved as if by magic when I open my eyes.

This darkness is terrible because there is no rest in it. The only thing I can do is list events that happened, and the hour, as the only proof I have. A statement of this kind is like a shield, even a weapon to place on the hand of justice, and ask, "How could the beautiful universe show me this ugly side? Is it necessary for the cosmic order that evil defiles me in this manner?"

At eleven twelve, I turn off the stick lamp. As if already waiting, Old Goat's quantum energy leaps. Or is it a darker reality, a black magic spirit dedicated to domination, without being seen, what's suddenly on top of my chest? He acts cute. *Hee-hee-hee.*

But I get up from bed, shake the covers, and call him abuser, trash, and monster. Probably he has not left the room, even after this tirade of hate, but there is silence.

A vibrating motion—not of love but of love's mocking—wakes me. They have accessed wirelessly—via invisible microphone—my pubic area, and AnnaLynn again enacts a masturbation scene, breathing hard and calling my name. I get up instantly and go to the small room to retrieve my plastic sack, my safety cover. The clock reads two fifty in the morning of the new day, February 27.

Light comes through the skylight, but it is still early. Something else besides the light awakes me. An *Ah-Oh*, as of pleasure, comes from between my legs. Junior, the promising future politician/lover, reenacts trauma by passing on the abuse, dressed in his ghost costume. I need to sleep. But the gang does not allow for so much freedom.

I get up from my mattress at five forty-two. I have not slept much. Just a few hours, snatched from Evil's persistence, will have to do for now---until the day of justice, of revelation, of release.

TWO

DANCING IN THE KITCHEN

Two cops bang on the door and ask me point-blank if I have any trouble with the neighbors. I have been dancing in the kitchen while sipping coffee with hair uncombed and no proper clothes on, celebrating I made it through the night. And what is more, this morning, because of the circumstances, the founder of the most famous budget counseling agency for the people in Monument has not tried to grab my behind virtually. So, I'm happy. It's better than following the mayor's advice and having myself be checked into a mental health care prison. I choose dancing.

I invite the officers into my attic, so they see I am busy writing and whatnot. They love the room. But business is business, and the more articulate of the two says, "Did you go out last night to paint something across the street?"

"I did."

I could hear the bullies breathing in my daring. They are in shock at the middle-class ghetto my street has become. Since when do we acknowledge what we do to others? We are an undistinguished blob of bodies that run outside as soon as it is dark to crouch under a fence, which is not our fence, to spy on the victim we have chosen, or someone has chosen for us. We cannot see anything but imagine terrible deeds committed under our noses, passing them as truths to justify more spying, as if our sins would somehow be necessary because of theirs. We introduce virtual reality in the form of parabolic microphones and micro-location quantum invisible travel into houses that are not ours and into which we have not been invited, to pass the night debasing someone and so feel our power.

We are so righteous. This new pastime brings a thrill into our existence it didn't have before. It is an insult to life itself, to principles, passion, hunger, and grief. They are all there, behind their darkened windows, betting this time the cops will take me away and they would have won finally. I can imagine the grins of expectation that my words bring to their plastic hearts.

The cops are fascinated.

"You did it? What did you do?"

"I wrote on a car's window with paint."

"Why did you do it?"

"I had to do something. I have reported this many times. The harassment must stop."

"What harassment? Something specific that happened."

"Two things yesterday. I was watching a movie in a room."

"The bedroom."

The specification by the police officer supports my suspicion that the bullies discuss, even with the police, in which room I am and what they think I do there, as if it were their business.

"It was, before. But now it is a room where I read and watch movies. At some point, I heard somebody was under my window, like they used to do before I installed cameras. I got up, the person started running away, and I saw him getting into his car, parked across from there. At full speed, noisy, it went up the hill, raging as usual. It was the son, Ferdinand Soto Jr., of number twenty-two. He has done it before, often after I turn off my lights."

"Why would he do this?"

"A group of people in the neighborhood engage in this behavior so they can drive me out. They have said it to my face. It's a hostile attitude they have, to support one another against one who may be different. And they have to trespass to do all these harassing actions."

"Do you have proof?"

"I have installed cameras, but they have learned to use the blind spots quite well. This path is narrow, and it's difficult to hide a camera. I have some recordings, but the police have ignored them in the past, as if they are not proof enough. For me, they are. I have seen them do it. They themselves talk about what they do."

"Then what happened?"

"I went on watching my movie, and I fell asleep about ten thirty."

"And then?"

"I was awakened by somebody muttering some words near my nose and laughing."

"You recognized the voice?"

"Yes."

"Was he there?"

"In some virtual-reality way, yes."

"Look, would you like us to refer you to a doctor at the hospital?"

"No, thank you. Your suggestion points to a feeling of impotence … I understand. And it may well be you have a concern for my health. But it also means that there is something you don't understand, and you reject educating yourself on the matter."

"Well, that's the first time I hear any of this. Do you know how weird it is?"

"I don't mean to be disrespectful, Officer, but you need to involve an expert in quantum physics, the same way other experts are involved in crime investigations."

"And what for? So that he tells us what happened?"

"That's not the function of an expert."

"Then?"

"To specify what can happen and can't happen in that … realm, reality."

I hear Hubber Dixon, an expert, repeating what I say behind his window. If I were he, I would have come out and said, "She is right; I will help." Are these first-class citizens? It seems the problems of society are not their problems, and they are not equal to everyone. They are superior. It may be that he can't come out and say, "Yes, this and that," without revealing his possible participation. Risking his neck. But it would save him in so many ways. I think Hubber has become the most vulnerable victim in this tragedy, and he does not know it. Yet he is silent. He is afraid, confused.

"That cannot happen. What you say is crazy."

"Well, I am here to help---not just in this case, but in any other similar. Just think, for identification of criminals, fingerprints are becoming almost obsolete. The side of the hand is the thing now because over 60 percent of crimes, including sexual crimes, are done virtually. And I know who is doing those on my street, and you do not wish to investigate them. Imagine if this were happening in an apartment building, where you don't know the people. It would be terrifying. I am so worried about the young! No one ready to help them!"

"I'll write it, thank you. Now we must see the family who reported you."

When they return, the two cute young policemen are in an aggressive mode, about to raid my home. They are demanding my identification, calling headquarters to see whether I had been busted for anything, like drugs, which is what the Sotos had told them. They ask if I would sign my statement.

"Yes, I stand by my word. After the second attack in my own home by Ferdinand Soto Jr. yesterday, being awakened by him after eleven by his virtual home invasion, I decided I had to do something. He and his father have been reported before, and nothing has been done. So, I am very conscious of what I am doing. I am trying, in a nonviolent way, to address their violence. I took a brush from my studio and black paint and wrote over his back window, 'Stop Harassment!'"

And I know I cannot call the authorities anymore to report what happened the night that followed, the terrible night of their revenge, and the next and the next that inevitably will happen, with the logic of the needs of the crazy for power, of the deranged. The police wouldn't understand, or they would be told not to understand. They probably would handcuff me and take me away to the station, as they promised, because I am bothering the nice Sotos once again.

At night, I'm not alone anymore. Even as early as the late afternoon, It creeps in close to where I am, as if crime itself suffered and must reach out for salvation. It's a terrible moment! Where will I hide? I am at the mercy of a shadow-directed force, hounding my body, like hunger a besieged city, invisible and inevitable. I feel the presence of Evil! Do I create this moment? Is it an intelligence outside myself, a trap activated by an unkind hand? Fate is materializing in my life, the irremediable, and its anguish stares at my desolation.

I am not ready for magic without ethics. Nobody should be. Let's all rebel in the name of the vulnerable, the broken, and the oppressed.

"Hello," says the voice casually.

What daring--- so stupid! Should I have felt flattered for having been chosen by It himself? Is this a sign of what absolute power could look like, not in a distant future, but now!?

"Hello" is all It said that night. But the presence stays, not quite knowing how to proceed. It stays, causing the space to feel swollen like an infected organ.

I have retreated to the little room, long ago built in the attic for the maid, to escape the others. This is the first night I had sensed that something truly unfamiliar to reason was happening, and if I hid in a corner far from whatever, I would be safe. But far from where? Fear and aloneness are fluid rivers; they can find the mysterious shrine of pain and hear the cry for help of our consciousness. The others cannot be reached. This panic cannot be communicated.

How exposed am I to the world, curled up on the armchair by the old desk, door and window locked! The lights are off. I am barely daring to breathe, a skill I have been practicing so often, that my belly has suffered—a protest nesting in my intestines, a great swelling pain. I am here because I have fled from other rooms. The last refuge reveals what is left of hope. Nothing.

I know the voice, and I could not think. I am just silent, as if accepting what is happening. Compliance with authority will save you, the presence of the Thing in my own room seems to demand. And in the street, just the day after the police were here, Soto Jr. spies on me relentlessly from his sports car, motor running. All the symbols of power are at his fingertips, as if his gasoline were paid by deep pockets, somebody else's pocket.

He beeps at me if I step out, and if my light goes on in the attic, he sends in a round glare through the window, circular like a huge, long-play record, that flies in and disappears, delivering a loud beep.

One of the many recordings the wireless abusers have in store is to be played at the push of a button. They have birds trapped, beating their wings; they let loose these sounds inside a closet or the room where I am. The sound goes off as suddenly as it started, leaving no trace of the violence. This is the perfect crime. You could have dreamt it.

And the following night, the thump of their GPS connection hits my northern window, a sign that they are coming. The cruel voice of the owner of the counseling place roars by my side, as if this were his bed.

"*¿Con quién?*"

With whom? With whom am I doing. What!?

There is an advantage, like a fleeting blessing in moments of abuse, that protects, as if it were not happening, as if you don't notice it has anything to do with you. If you were to tell someone, they would say, "Are you stupid or what? Do you think everything in life is fun? Sometimes you meet jerks. Just don't be so thin-skinned." And more frequently now, they say, "That's crazy. It cannot happen."

You blank out. You forget to breathe. If you do, you make the hurt yours. And if you don't, you can't forget the fright---just fright, without a story to go with it.

And so, you describe actions in the physical world. You tell of Soto Jr. and how at five in the afternoon or ten or eleven at night, he comes into your driveway, into the little path under your window, and crouches there grinning and laughing, away from the camera. Suddenly, he springs up, laughing loudly for the benefit of his audience, and jumps in his sports car. Beeping loudly, he speeds up the hill, as if something about you warrants this public ridicule every afternoon and every night, for eternity.

Later, as their kinky sex vocabulary for spooky happenings nearby grew, and Soto Jr. would get ready to go to important meetings, he would access my room after the energy signal hitting the window, grab me by the shoulder and around the breast very tightly, as with a strap. He then released my body with contempt, press my belly with his teleportation fist, and then jump into his sports car, driving at full speed, honking in triumph into success.

One thing is clear: they always know where I am.

Old Goat starts approaching me slowly, emphasizing the strength of his invisible presence, throwing his hot breath onto my face, and then pushing my back. It's only noon, impressing carefully in my awareness the joining forces of time and terror. I pretend I don't know what's going on. This is what I'm always told: don't notice. But I realize too late that approach is a mistake now.

THREE

RAFI SALCEDO MISSES THINGS

Officer Green behaves quite unconcerned for a policeman, unconcerned completely. *Heartless really*, thinks Rafi Salcedo, *as if he's decided he doesn't give a banana because that's what the system expects of him.* If you want to convince him of a law violation, bring him a stiff body. Otherwise, you are out of luck.

There he is, coldly looking at the distressed young woman who had taken the trouble of writing all about some trespassers, three pages with dates, names, and details. Has Rafi seen her before? Green—short, chubby, and unfeeling, mumbles, not looking at her but at some important greasy spot by the garbage container while specifying that the criminal must be on the premises when police arrived. It's like telling the creep up the hill who is trespassing and breaking the gate's lock, "Just wait here for the police."

"Or don't bother calling," says Officer Green once again, raising his voice.

And nobody objects.

Plenty of guys in uniform wandering like lost souls around the hallway, but not one tells Green, "Listen here. What are you being paid for? Help her! Do something."

The "Defund the Police" movement has a point. Unless you are a protected criminal, they have no use for you, but you could drop by anytime you need an insult to make you feel better. What a culture! Satisfied they are, with groans, grins, and idle hands around their well-fed waists.

Rafi Salcedo misses things. He feels he was becoming a member of the disaffected, the un-rebelled backward army of workplace cranks. But why? What does he need to bring back his former happiness? He had been happy---once. He misses it there, near his heart, inspiring his thoughts and making him look forward to the next minute with memories of yesterday. He arrives now by three o'clock sharp on Mondays, and flabby, like Green. What a thought! Couldn't he do better to entertain himself?

Somebody had suggested this change of schedule. When he asked who, eyes went straight to that clever space in the infinite corner of the room, where one retreats to avoid the responsibility of an answer. It was envy. Rafi was not to be allowed the freedom he had enjoyed when he was an undercover cop. They needed him on the street. Whenever a non-English resident called, they told him. Yeah, right.

But to hell with it. He wouldn't give them the pleasure of contemplating sorrow seething. He was a principled man; there was a structure to his life that you just couldn't mess up so easily. Somebody walked in. What was his name?

"So, Mr. Sheriff, no divorce papers to serve today?" the man addresses Rafi warmly.

"No, we live in the most harmonious moment of civilization. No frying pan flying across the kitchen this morning! How are you, senior guy? You must be reaching retirement age fast."

"Don't wanna think about it. I moved. There's bills to pay. What else!"

And the guy sighs. There's nothing much to talk about. Now Rafi remembers what he was called, "The Pig." His abusers baptized him this way, and it stuck in the wider world, as if goodness were not to be counted in a man's life, just the put-downs.

"You moved? Isn't that what your abusers wanted? Why give them the pleasure?"

"I know what you mean. But life's short. I would arrive home after ten hours in this joint and find four luxury cars parked across the street. The woman owner of the place never worked a day since I've known her but paid cash. And I have reported the tree I planted myself mysteriously destroyed and azalea plants, all my vegetation, trampled on. Every time I reported them, the so-called neighbors laughed. Brought along one more shiny car with tinted glass. As soon as I arrived, one of them stepped out and hollered, 'Boys, you behave now! The Pig is home. He will call the police, you know.'"

"The police did nothing."

"Yes, it did. Protected them. Didn't have enough proof they had done it was the verdict. That's what the town police said. There was even a video, but apparently it wasn't what's accepted as proof."

"Sorry. I wish we could do something to help."

"What can a good person do when confronted by an evil system? Just look at Green, the crime prevention officer. He only moves when someone is killed."

"What can I say? He's not especially friendly to me, even when I resolved for him the mystery of the Fort Provision drug murder. But I saw him running around this morning as if with a purpose."

"Haven't you heard? A seventeen-year-old was found shot on Garfield early this morning."

"I feel awful! And not for the boy! Well, yes, for him. But also for some degradation nesting in me, sitting here feeling sorry for myself, ruminating on some lost freedom, while a boy met death on the trampled snow of a forsaken street at dawn!"

"Don't feel too bad, Salcedo. We all do it, worrying about our contracts and retirements without even asking first whether we did anything to save a life. You are not the worst among us. At least you mourn!"

"Yes, I mourn, if that could help! And yet these are unavoidable crimes. There is nobody here with a purpose or plan to change anything. That's the trouble."

"Oh, I agree that having a person of quality at the top would make a difference in many ways. But these crimes, would they remain or push the pain someplace else? Having more police around would perhaps prevent what? Don't you believe in the great purpose of our profession?"

"Sure, I do. We are outdated, though. We need to redefine our field of action, along with our mission. We cannot continue being a punitive organization in today's world."

"I sort of see it your way, like when I lived in that house with the garden I loved. I should have been helped to stay there."

"Yeah. That is so unfortunate, how the little Hitlers keep pushing us around! But these deaths---of someone who is not even a man yet, in a street where the heads of families are working twelve hour-shifts for a pay that is not enough or are in jail or somewhere else but helping that youth, who is out there hustling for territory, power, money, pot, or love. And he is not equipped for the struggle. Can you help there essentially?"

"You know, Salcedo, you see things. I understand how you solve cases that no one can begin to crack. I never understood before. They should let you have your own schedule back. Somebody doesn't want you to discover something. If you want to know what I think, you have my vote if you fight this. You should."

"Thank you. I really appreciate it.

And Rafi Salcedo stands up and approaches The Pig, not just to be polite but to shake his hand and thank him with his name attached to the big thank you. Yeah, he remembers his real name now, Tom Fink. There's a funny story having to do with that name. They would tell it around here. But now jokes are not cool. They could get you in trouble for a reason you couldn't have guessed.

"Thank you for stopping by, Tom. Let's talk some more about how we can save the world."

At the door, they laugh as they part, a happy laugh. Rafi Salcedo feels uplifted by the freshness of the exchange with Tom. Not everyone has become detached with that modern aloofness that deprives situations of a moral reason for the involvement of the individual citizen, the "I'm not to blame" culture.

Thinking all this reminds Rafi of the file that Sister Marisol from Saint Augustine had left with him when she parted for the missions at the Mexican border. He misses her, the light of her presence, the authority with which she demanded respect for everything for everyone. That file had to be read to bring the suffering of the forgotten close to the hungry heart, to reveal the innocence of the desperate.

COFFEE

FOUR

THE BILL OF RIGHTS— INSPIRED NEW NEIGHBOR

It, the owner or former owner of the people's counseling place in Monument, was not the original bodiless ghost. Hubber Dixon, new to number twenty-one, was. Or that's what I thought. He had that clean-cut, army-protected presence of the veteran, the recent recruit, the rule-and-discipline-driven subject. I was delighted there was a military man next door! The bullies were about to see what a Bill of Rights–inspired neighborhood looked like, a man with a civics education, I guessed.

I decided then and there to invite him to coffee. As I stepped out for my morning walk to the beach, I saw the man called Hubber, my then-possible savior, noiselessly closing his car door. He had gadgets for everything to work silently, except the grass cutter and leaf blower. The latter he would use at night later to wake me up. When he became the willing bully gang's next victim, without his understanding, for he was far more vulnerable than I was.

"Are you the new neighbor?"

Boy wasn't I charming and upbeat!

"Yes, glad to meet you. In fact, I was thinking the other day I should go up to your door and introduce myself."

"Great! Let's have coffee sometime. Let me write my email here. There are some agreements we can make to take care of the vegetation along the border that could save us time, if we do it together!"

"Perfect. Here is my email."

He could surely be a gentleman.

"Yes, let's share information because I had a lot of difficulty with the man from whom I bought the house."

Incredible! I thought, very pleased to see he had a story to share.

The day we discussed the first complaint to the city, which was against Hubber, the mayor and his right-hand man exclaimed at the same time, "And she tried to warn him!" I did. But he was not the listening kind. He made the same mistake whenever the occasion required that he take a different approach. It always got him into trouble, as if he could not outgrow some trauma.

Hubber may have shared experiments or fun tricks to be accepted into the tough environment, being college-educated--- a liability next to the other guys who had been living in the ghetto. It was a form of bonding with the men, now that he had stuff they could value.

Once, away for a while from a work trip with the River Guards, he came back with a bunch of guys and one girl. They hid away in strict silence for special whole-night quantum parties. In the span of the three or four days that lasted the Thanksgiving vacation, the girl went from being a jeering bully crouching behind the fence laughing in the dark, to hiding from me in fear or shame.

I think she had come before with other people, all with expensive cars, not of subtle construction but the swollen, shiny, aggressive design loved by the emerging middle class. The first time I was aware of her, I put up curtains in the window facing Hubber's raised uncovered porch. I went to the desk next to this window and caught sight of him saying something into her ear, and they both came quite close, stopped by my fence, pushed it, and laughed. It was a miracle this fence was still standing. He had been kicking it nightly since he joined the bullying neighbors. The guy was angry at something. Now there were curtains all over, the way things were in besieged territory. How disturbing! This uncivility disguised as patriotism!

They partied in the long room on the opposite side; sometimes one of the cars silently left in the middle of the night. Then they came back, more silently if possible. Sunday afternoon of that wordless party weekend, I was sitting typing by the desk under the skylight and felt fog hands reaching my backside, on top of each hip, so subtle, like cat paws without the nails, and warm, too. I had experienced them before. Hubber had quite a touch. I glanced out of the window, and behind a canvas panel, I saw a beam of light. He was showing off his experiment, no doubt. It was sort of illegal maybe, but he was proud of it.

I sat back, and yes, they were doing something over my body with the warm, invisible fog hands. I remembered the Halloween toy I had bought to play with when I wanted to tell someone in his loop that I knew what they were doing. It always put them off--- the one with the *Ghostbusters* music theme. So, I sprang up, opened the window, and let loose those plastic little ghosts, while playing

Something's weird in the neighborhood!
Who you gonna call?
Ghostbusters!

The fog magic stopped. I could hear the bunch gasp behind the now-dark canvas panel. One by one, the cars left silently, except the woman's, who stayed until dark. She opened her car door and, looking down the hill toward my window, laughed unpleasantly. There was no joy, no music, and no audible conversations, just plans, schedules, projects, or experiments, like this crazy quantum invisible matter house invasion. They were tricks to fill the emptiness.

But on Thursday a few weeks later, arriving home after dark, I saw her directing a car coming down the hill, from a microphone behind the big, dark window in the computer room. With a rough, unpleasant voice, she directed the driver to park closer to my house. A hedge was there, so the car would be hidden from me. This was a warning that something was cooking in Hubber's computer laboratory.

I turned off my lamp after watching *Crime and Punishment's* ending once again, when Rodion and Sonya entered Petrovich's office to confess and thus start on the road to salvation. I always cry here. How I envy their innocence and their love! Redemption! There is nothing but light afterward. *Stay there!* I tell myself, wishing my own life could be part of that story.

The thump on the window glass followed, as if the lamp going to sleep and The Monster commencing his ghoulish ritual were two consecutive beats of the Heart of Darkness coming to devour me. I heard his difficult, coarse breathing. I had thought at times that he could be ill, and all this modern galaxy travel was undermining his health. But I had also thought, and often, that he may think he is attracting passion this way through terror, not love.

He was in the middle of the room, approaching the bed where I was trying to rest, coming closer with his disgusting breathing tactics, feeling the blankets at the far end of the futon to find me. I moved and covered my head. I had thought at first that I was found through my breathing, and I had been sleeping with a scarf around the middle of my face. Scary, waking up while feeling there was no air. I did give up this way of protecting myself. It never worked. I was found no matter what I did.

The Monster was nervous tonight, pushing my foot with his invisible pointed wire, as if he wanted to place my leg in a way he likes it better. But I didn't let him. Raging he was because I fought back. I felt his stupid invisible weight on my left leg, and he pushed my arm down the way he had done before in a brutal maneuver; he was trying to dominate me by holding me down---what a rapist would do, freezing my arm in the process. I moved away and called him disgusting, moron, abuser, and son of the devil---all those things one would not say in other moments in polite company.

Talking to him, something that I just found that works, deactivated him instantly. I went downstairs and made tea and sipped it, hiding behind a door in the room where Unk's music was stored. I breathed quietly; afraid he would find me, my body tense.

I didn't know how long I spent this way, sipping tea without making noise, behind a door. Eyes wide-open to the dark, afraid. I asked myself what I was going to do. Sometimes I dwelt on possible plans to make the situation public, such as painting some boards and sitting myself with them by the Soto curbstone: THIS MAN IS A VIRTUAL-REALITY RAPIST. JUSTICE TO VICTIMS!!!! Or something of the sort.

Of course, the police would come and arrest me for inciting violence, loitering, or being crazy. That, if friends of Ferdinand Soto Jr., who stayed in apartments down the road, didn't roll me over with their cars before the police arrived.

Or I could make things simpler for myself, buying a spray can and painting RAPIST all over his house. I would be arrested, but this crime would go public. I mused often whether someone would press for it to get investigated. The last thing I should do was to lose faith.

I dreamt with finding a solution to this nightmare. I moved when my feet started getting cold. Should I go back upstairs to the attic? I decided to stay in the old bedroom, on the bunch of cushions and blankets I prepared to be comfortable while reading books and watching movies. No room in my home was private anymore. They all had a window facing the house of one in the bully-gang, whose members had fashioned a space cut in hedges and fences where they could gather with their friends and spy on me. They had figured out how to be invisible to cameras and share information on the alternative spaces, those with lots of vegetation and blind spots.

Anything I did, or better, what they invent that I do or did or didn't do, is a matter for laughter and ridicule, for public shaming. Even my little flip cell phone wasn't private. I placed a vitamin order from a discount place, and of course Soto heard it all from his bugging cell. He brought Emmett by my fence, and both laughed. The next day, I got a call from a number that turned out to be a fake Medicare number. Soto Jr. was saying *Da-Da-Da*, mimicking my speech while his friends at the barber's roared next to him. He hung up. I called back, and he had blocked my number already. He had done this before. I called from the home number, not the cell, and an ad from Medicare sounded in the recording, "You can get vegetables and other food for free." But it was not a real government number. The communication stopped there. There was nowhere to call, nowhere to reach out. He was using their goodwill to insult somebody.

Sleep cuddled me in no time in the faraway room, which had the disadvantage of being next to the porch, in direct hearing line from Emmett and Betty. But they must be asleep or at least not alerted of my presence, because all the lights were off. Now that I had no privacy, the minutes in which I was not attacked were like being in paradise.

I woke up in the night and I was not alone. I was so tired. Why didn't they let me sleep? I noticed that the fog hand, with a defined point or finger—that's how I perceive it—had been touching or massaging the space between the bone under my neck and my breast, and not in an aimless way. Well-thought-out, careful, and professional. Didn't rush or missed an inch, as if there was a defined end or objective, and the fog hand knew how to get there.

This was not It, the impatient brute who discarded his stinking breath on my face as his macho right. No, this was different. One was an object. I was. From the distance of a laboratory, they were experimenting on you, on me. The fog hand followed a well-researched route. I felt it knew my body like a lover, as if it had been there before. It went down to my belly slowly, without hurry. It massaged it, going around in circles, as if making sure my digestion was in order.

But I moved. All stopped. Nobody was in this refuge of mine---my little cushion-made bed with old blankets---but the night and me. I was so tired; I couldn't move more. I felt I needed sleep so badly. I dozed. The fog hand did know when I was asleep.

I woke up again with the belly massage about to end, and I turned around facedown, as if for protection. But the fog hand was ready for any contingency. Using something pointed, it felt like a needle was thrust into my behind. The fog hand seemed to have arrived at some climax. But I was afraid of what happened next. I got up.

I remembered the car that the woman had directed to park in a secluded space. I looked out of the front window because something could be seen from there. It was still there. I could make out half of the trunk space, a dark color, maybe blue, a party of some kind, something planned, an experiment, a bet, accomplishments in the world of strange quantum effects, secrets among the initiated few: something to brag about in the silence of the night, frightened it would come out and so lose the forbidden pleasure of the thrill---or maybe it compromised their professionalism.

I heated water for coffee without turning on the kitchen lights, just using the stove clock clarity to move around. The world was empty. This must be how the imprisoned felt, the abandoned. In a silent world made up of their bodies, which they didn't own, and the will of that invisible force rushing to abuse. Your feelings didn't count. You were an object, dehumanized, marginalized, and without rights. How to live?

I went by the front door on my way to the studio, to find peace there now that the night was ending. The car was gone. All was planned, now finished.

But I didn't know what happened. At different times in the next days, I got glimpses of the young woman, with the look of someone who had become brutal out of fear or guilt. She was cutting grass with one of the noisy Hubber's gadgets, and when she saw me, she almost lost her balance in her hurry to hide. There were no more parties.

Reviewing one of my cameras, I saw that around Sunday, very early, like four in the morning, the garage door opened noiselessly. Her car came out. That party, to which she guided someone, did make an impact on her soul. But I cannot know anything really at all about those who do not speak.

How did Hubber feel about all this? He must have found balance for his own life in these happenings, a balance I couldn't imagine, a sense of power, of control. Did the Old Monster teach him something of his invisibility black magic tricks? Or was this a quantum leap experiment? Was he thinking at all beyond the pleasure of turning matter invisible and cooling atoms to temperatures comparable to interstellar vacuum to see what happened when you came in contact this way with a woman's body?

If I could not imagine something essential about Hubber and the Sotos, I would be terrified. There are two hands holding my behind while I cut up fruit for breakfast, which I detested. I fought them, moving around, kicking the empty air. But later, there were the playful invisible legs that went up and down my attic stairs while I read on the futon---legs imitating my own steps, pretending to dance when they arrived at the top. Something endearing and cute in this madness.

This invisible world is like the Blake's poem about the Creator, made up of playfulness and evil.

The other night, it was something like a bird inside the small room, hitting the walls again and again, so I had to go to sleep downstairs. As soon as I left, no more bird was heard.

One appearance of the bodiless Hubber I cut short, and I felt sorry afterward I missed that experience. But for safety's sake, one cannot be a witness to all these wonders, to this spiritual new challenge. I had turned off the lights; my eyes truly were tired. I wanted rest so badly! Then a breeze started dancing over my face, lightly, almost lovingly. What a nice way to go to sleep, an equestrian lullaby. It was just the feeling, with no words to destroy the harmony or sound to disturb the peace. Then the breeze concentrated on the left cheek, just over the mouth, close to the nose. It was such a pleasurable feeling. I could not accuse Hubber of not knowing the human body, how to awaken it. But probably he could not do it with his own hands because this would require responsibility, communication, or love.

Thinking all this, I sensed movement toward me, solid, with structure, as if it were a real body with a magnetic field. But I knew a body could not fly the space between two houses and come in through the wall. *Not even Hubber could achieve this*, I thought.

I turned the light on and sat up on the futon. The movement stopped. I sensed a kind of perfection had been achieved here. And having it too close, in the darkness, I thought it could be dangerous. What would it want of me? I remembered the day when Soto Jr. called the police when I had written "Stop the Harassment" on his luxury car window. The officers inquired about this invisible home invasion and asked, probably as a joke, whether I thought this ghost would be dangerous.

I could hear Hubber, glued to the window next to mine, breathing in hard when I answered that I used to think this would not be dangerous—beyond the scare of being touched by handless hands and spoken by mouths you cannot see—but that I had changed my mind. It could be dangerous.

My throat and my eyes had been attacked by a pointed thing when Soto was angry, when I reported him to the police. Whatever the thing he used was, it hurt, and I closed my eyes and moved the head in case it could do harm in the material world. Black magic's rage was a never-ending need for revenge.

One night, I had made my bed on a rug near the noisy refrigerator so The Monster could not find me through my breath. But he found me and stuck two pointed, bodiless objects in my ears. That hurt. He did it several times, trying to make me lose my balance. Once, it was by covering my ears as I stood by the bathroom mirror while combing my hair. But I moved away. I already knew the tricks, until the electrical shock treatments started. But that came much later.

Proving that this state-of-the-art crime was going on, staged by such respectable people as the owner of a people's counseling place and a future elected official, seemed impossible. The lack of sleep and the tension had damaged my digestive system so I could hardly eat anything that was not boiled pumpkin, so as not to suffer from swelling, diarrhea, and nausea. The first time I thought I could just prove something, no matter how remotely, I grabbed it.

Desperation can bring one to strange situations. The night in question, I had brought my movable bed to the little attic room, the most remote in the house: if the mailman and his boyfriend were not in and therefore not waiting behind the hedge for me to turn off my light so they could start to descend into the deep, debased world of vulgar insult, I was safe for a few hours.

They were not in the house down the street. But Hubber was, right on the other side. As soon as I had fallen asleep, he woke me up by hitting the drum of my left ear. I was sure there was a visible injury. It was close to midnight, but it could be worth it to go to the emergency room at the hospital and talk it over with a doctor.

What could I lose? I got dressed quickly in new clean clothes. I didn't realize until I was sitting in the makeshift provisional waiting room among the barely dressed regular patients how out of place I must have looked. I was healthy, well-dressed, and probably wealthy. What was I doing there? I gave my name and insurance card to the man behind a portable check-in structure and sat down to wait. I didn't know the hospital was doing so many renovations. *The emergency room didn't need them*, I thought.

But the feeling of despair and insomnia hung over the work-in-progress. Road work lights shone everywhere. Old doors were blocked. Short, detour-like passageways made it confusing to find the entrance to the check-in point. Out-of-shape nurses, probably changing shifts, were standing by bundles of sheetrock and pipes, smoking and talking to security guards and swollen men with hard hats. This could be anywhere in the middle of nowhere, a factory or low-income apartment complex starting to change something to cover helplessness and lack of vision.

Nobody talked. What was there to say? Language creates worlds, and all the waiting patients had was silence, pain, addiction, and poverty in plain sight. What could they say? Maybe they were looking for more opioids to get them through the night.

A huge color screen was playing in front of me. I scanned the room, and nobody was looking, but whoever had put the TV there had a point. Without its gaudy color and inappropriate message, sitting in that waiting room would be unbearable. One would start looking at the pain and distress on the patients' faces, even hearing their sorrow and desperation.

Finally, a nurse called me in. She took my temperature and vital signs, almost perfect. She found my file in the computer, where it is written I don't take medication, and I am a vegetarian who takes her turmeric supplements seriously. This, I guess now looking back, was weird to start with. Who had heard of anyone who did not take any drugs, not even aspirin? She asked me why I had come in.

"I have pain in my left ear. I want to see if the doctor can find any injury, even the smallest trace of it."

"What did you do to hurt it?"

Of course, she took down what followed at great speed. The woman looked radiant, excited. She had something special! I said two neighbors were intruding in my home, using some wireless mechanism, a sort of micro-location device and a parabolic microphone to listen in.

"And that's how your ear was hurt?"

"I think so. It's hard to believe, but some gadgets, or scientific experiments, now allow for those things to happen."

"I get it. Well, you wait outside for the doctor to call you."

And I waited until well past one in the morning, sitting by myself on a plastic chair while looking at the obscene program the big-screen TV played. It was a video advertising a budget vacation on some island, with a swimming pool and plenty of empty chairs, touching one another to fit in lots of people. There was a long table with an all-you-can-eat buffet, a smiling woman sunning herself by the pool, and a smiling waiter bringing her a long, pink drink. What would the awareness of this plastic paradise do on the consciousness of these indigent people sitting next to me? Were they watching? Did they think this ad was directed at them? Were they included in any program, other than this precariousness, this waiting, this destiny as passive clients?

Sometime in the aimless night of the disenfranchised, where nothing happened, a young employee not wearing the nurse uniform of the hospital showed up. She was uncomfortable, snakelike in movements; she wasn't sure where the person she was looking for was. She stopped by my chair and asked me if I was the professional in charge of a woman sitting nearby. I told her I was waiting for the doctor to attend to me. I had been there for over one hour. She realized I was the person she was looking for, only that I didn't look like the person she thought she was looking for.

I followed her, and she kept asking me whether I was familiar with the place. I thought she meant the emergency room. Sure, I had been there with my late uncle several times. But I could see by her body language—tense, watchful, and frightened—that I had not understood her. We arrived at a small room where four large, uniformed guards waited for me. They asked me to put my hands up and checked my body for weapons.

"What is this?"

The men looked at me, ashamed. "I think we made a mistake," one said.

Two of them retreated, leaving there two female guards and the young woman. The guards searched my purse and my jacket pockets.

All seemed confused. If they could, they would say they were sorry. But they were at work. This is what they had been instructed to do.

"I just came to have my ear looked at. It hurts."

The young woman finally decided to let me go. "Must have been a mistake. Wait here and the doctor will see you soon."

They really changed this hospital, no question, with new management and a new order. It looked chaotic in that emergency room where Unk had been well attended. To my right, there were rooms locked and windows covered. I could hear the useless complaints of the abandoned and damned and a nurse yelling at someone to get the needle to inject another shot. The row of computers behind the counter were attended by women surrounded by wires and printers. They stood up, went for a bottle of water, and stopped to talk to somebody in the back for what looked like an excessive amount of time. They were bored. I tried to get the attention of one of these women, but no one was available. Their eyes were open wide, looking here and there, without aim.

Just then, I saw the nurse and approached her to ask what was happening. She tried to avoid me, running away. She said she was busy. She went to the counter with the aimless women and the computers and said something, pointing at me. They all looked at me in shock. The ER manager also came out from his office to look at me, laughing.

When the nurse was close enough for me to talk, I said her behavior was unacceptable. She tried to avoid me but said, "That thing you said about the ear was crazy."

"It is not your function to make that decision. You just refer me to the doctor. You should be reported for your unprofessional behavior." I said that, but I realized she was not worried, not in this place.

I waited for the doctor, but after more than forty minutes, I realized he was not coming, for whatever reason. I left the hospital, without proof that the virtual-reality bullies had damaged my ear, but with a clearer understanding of the dangers of my plight.

There was some damage in my left ear, but I didn't push for any proof the police could use. The private doctor I went to said it was because I eat almonds, which are hard. I must go on a soft diet, bananas and mashed potatoes. He, of course, could read what the ER nurse wrote and looked at me quizzically, wondering if a doctor saw me. I said no, which was true. I explained the decadence I saw in the new ER. One sees more poverty there now than one used to. He looked at me sideways as he brought me to the receptionist with my folder.

I had the injury, but not a sympathetic doctor willing to listen and be a witness. Everyone washed their hands. They didn't want to join the ranks of the suspected.

FIVE

FEAR BRINGS LIBERATION

"Fear, finally!"

Rafi Salcedo remembers Renata exhaling those words as a liberation when she saw the neighbors turning off their lights as he arrived at her door. It's odd that the negative could bring such hope. But Rafi understands. He himself had suffered from bigotry ever since he could remember his own life as an individual: literally physically pushed, set aside, belittled, and made to feel less than nothing; existing and seen but wronged and worthless, without a right to speech. So, what could Renata do but be pleased when she saw that her strategy brought about relief?

He wants to say, *Good for you!* But he's a cop and a professional. His smile speaks for him, though, and he knows that Renata guessed he was on her side, making him happy.

Salcedo was from around here, but no one remembered him as far as he could tell, not that he tried connecting with any organization or looking up old friends. It all felt different, as if everybody had moved out, removing all the memories like useless furniture, memories as disconnected burdens, triumphs, and regrets, amounting to nothing. And he, an impostor, a failure hounding a living from the shadows, was back in the old town, as if there were not world enough somewhere else far away.

The old Rafi is still here after all, he thinks, *dragging around a life that contemplates the impossible.* Could he change his inadequacies or at least forget all that had happened---his shyness, that brought about so much contempt; the accent his mother had not managed to erase and because of which he refused to say a word in case he sounded like her; the basic ugliness of his being; the chubby body frozen by cold and shyness, bound in that eternal brown sweater?

Rafi believes he still looked the same, because childhood shame can't be erased by age and respectability, and any healing that could exist has shunned him ever since, like love.

He always ends these thoughts with the "like love" refrain, because they would not feel complete otherwise. That's what his mother told him at times. He was not good enough for important things, no doubt because she herself felt unworthy of things like love. And once that he had humbled himself enough with these memories, he could put them aside for a while, until he wanted something badly enough, like what's-its-name. Yes, love.

Bars, churches, dances, and committees, he doesn't show up to any event or celebration. Why bother? But he knows of their existence; he must, it's part of his job. He avoids them. Rafi tells himself there is nothing he wanted to say. So why risk going into places and situations that would clearly bring sadness? Because he had tried. He tried so hard that he was even married once.

"Who owns this car? Are you Dora Ortiz? Are you allowed to live here?"

At nine in the evening and in this rude manner, Rafi Salcedo introduces himself to Renata. Boy, did he feel out of place! Now, he stands in front of her, smiling and full of light, receiving the brutal indignity of the police barging into her space. Once he barks those official indiscretions, Rafi feels unworthy of his badge. But he stands there stupidly despite having questioned her human rights by his very presence.

"Would you like to come in?"

"No. I'm fine here." Rafi Salcedo is secretly filming the exchange. *Pornographer!* He kicks himself in silence. *Jerk! Nincompoop.*

"Well, I do not know who Ortiz is. I bought the car two years ago. I know it had another owner before, but here is my registration."

"Driver's license and insurance all in order?"

Rafi doesn't know how they got the Ortiz name involved, but clearly the guys in Traffic had not checked everything. *So responsible!* he thinks. And he's videotaping her, without her knowing, by orders of the chief of police, meaner by the day to honest women since an honest policewoman reported him for harassment at the job. And the city had to pay four-hundred-thousand-dollars. No problem.

This is not fair, damn it! We live in a corrupt world, and I contribute to corruption's victory with my silence. I am an ally of evil. A moral failure, you, Rafi!

"Yeah, I see all's in order, madam. And you…are you allowed to live here in this house?"

Renata smiles at the question, and suddenly she knows why he had banged at her door in the dark, as if addressing a criminal. The disrespect is prominent here, a right exercised by the right kind of people. In fact, she had been hearing Betty in the garden, pushing Hubber, the new neighbor, to call the police and report her.

"Sure. It is mine."

He does not have a response to this. How insane of him to put himself and this woman in this situation by order of the chief of police, on a tip by the neighbors!

"Say, are you having problems with anyone 'round here? Do you get along?"

"I get along with those who want to get along with me."

"Yeah. I see that."

"Sure."

"Do you write any emails to them?"

"I have written to one."

"Don't write anymore."

"I wrote to one who gave me his address and said to write if there were any issues."

"What issues?"

"He cut my vegetation without my permission and dumped it in my garden. Then he destroyed an attachment to a fence and trespassed. And kicks the fence—"

"Why didn't you report it to the police?"

"I did."

"What did they do?"

"Nothing."

"Well, if that's the case, it cannot be prosecuted under our laws. But don't write to the neighbor anymore."

"And what do I do if he keeps trespassing?"

"Just don't write to him."

"Officer, I thank you so much for coming. This issue is now in the hands of the city. It will be resolved. Have a great evening. Peace."

And Rafi Salcedo, the fair policeman, the public servant on the side of the voiceless and the oppressed, the silent one who could not be bought nor corrupted, doesn't even have a good night for this woman. And she had said "Peace." He almost trips while walking toward the car backward, in a daze. He feels more than useless. He's an impostor.

Rafi, you are wasting your life. What will you do to win your self-respect back?

These are not neighbors; the woman is right. And he himself is a failure.

You, failure! Fracaso, y del malo! El peor. ¡Abandonar a una mujer!

Salcedo could have said, "I'm a failure" or "I have failed." But to personalize his self-disgust, he is not ready for that responsibility; it makes him afraid, soiled, at a loss. The way he had expressed himself, he could imagine it was happening to another person.

He drove away to file the report in a sort of lucid trance, as if he really intended to do something else. Like an automaton, he took the next call. He finished helping at the ball court behind the hospital, an old story as well. It didn't welcome a solution, not the way the dispute was designed. The lady in one of the houses didn't want that ball court with a bunch of Latinos playing there, dark, muscular, sweaty, and beautiful. The men played, regardless of her opinion, more and more of them for longer hours, as if this insistence had to happen as an answer to the woman's opposition.

The lady often called the police if it got dark and the guys were still playing, although the host also owned a house, and the court was his backyard. The lady didn't like this. The ball game host was not deterred by the woman's unrest, even less after she complained to the city council. It was a war zone now. Neither one of them had the Constitution in mind. They were not equals. Each one wanted to prevail over the other.

At first, it seemed to Salcedo that the Latino players had been wronged, victimized. But he didn't know what to think when the games went on after ten and midnight, and at three in the morning, players kept swarming in, hoping for hot fun.

"What a waste!"

Despite the sordidness of the stories and as the night advances, Rafi felt lighter. Something had started to change. *Una nueva vida.* This new life stuff sounded strange, because at the nice woman's house, that Renata, he was kicking himself every two minutes. *Bum! Paid bully at the harassers' service!*

She had explained herself well despite having an accent like his mother's. It's funny that he would remember this now, with longing and a smile. Truly new. Something essential had changed, and he was ready to forgive his mother for unresolved stuff and baggage.

The family had gone through so much because of those accents, which implied other differences, those inadequacies that others perceived. And in the present here, at the time of maturity and progress, someone else right in the same town was being tortured, like his mother had been.

We don't evolve; this is certain.

Going back to the happiness part. What he had felt while facing the calm woman was real. He liked whatever it was. He wanted to sink his teeth into the feeling, bite, taste a chunk of the wonderful light it could bring to his bleak existence, if he dared.

It is as if we, the bulk of the people, thought these bigotry issues were a thing of the past. We don't have the guts to have difficult conversations, and let poor women like Ranata deal with the racists alone. Who cares! This is not supposed to be happening, so she must have done something to bring it along. What's wrong with us? Where are we headed? We grow out of resolving, clarifying and making difficult choices. But we are looking the other way. Cowards! I wonder what she's feeling now---what wouldn't I give to know!

One thirty in the morning. Notes on the unexpected pleasurable.

An unnatural air blows on my nose, and I wake up. The window near me is closed. There are two walls between my face and another window, and it's one thirty in the morning on a calm spring night. I thought right away that Betty had hit on another way of waking me up, tired of pretending to be a mourning dove. *The stupid old bag!* It's the most logical thought, besides the possibility of my being crazy.

I forget about this event. There's no space in my burdened spirit for another experience of this unexplainable sort. But this is the start of Hubber's virtual presence. I had invited him to coffee to warn him of what could happen if the culture doesn't change, but he cannot understand that he is more vulnerable than I am. Those who pretend to be his friends and welcome him would be the ones to put him in danger. So, this invisible presence is somehow his way of coming close to me, although maybe he doesn't understand what his needs and his traumas do to the actions he takes---his traumas, and the fear of being associated with the outcast.

I cannot respond to what they do to me in an effective manner, even if I tried. I am not one of them. And they don't want clarifications, working out a way of doing things convenient for everyone. They can do what they please, if I am here---and anywhere else for that matter. The Sotos had my biometrics recorded by their machines. They can find me among the crowds, far away, anywhere.

SIX

FIRST COFFEE WITH RAFI SALCEDO

"Yes, I have thought about what could be going inside these men and in AnnaLynn, who is there all the time, getting her slice of sick pleasure on the sly, risking all if they get caught? Must be something important that is lacking, maybe some burdensome secret from the past or a misunderstanding of how to heal the suffering of being. But, you know, I don't think they are afraid. They cannot be caught."

Nata--as Officer Rafi Salcedo, inviting a client to coffee on his day off proposed to call her-- is careful. Not only is this man, through one of those necessary accidents, one of the most understanding cops that came to her house, but she had the extra good luck of bumping into him at the supermarket. Her angels must have created that galactic euphoria. Unk was still watching over her! She'd had time to reign in her emotions. So, she's careful; it's better to show her intellectual, philosophical side than look paranoid.

"I'm glad you are doing that kind of thinking for all the reasons in the world. The most important one, because their treatment of you is the result of their fear, of envy. You are so different from them, so educated! You look well-off. It is like the old scene at recess hour in high school. The loud losers isolating the good student and doing silly things to put her down. These things hurt, but they are not important."

"You are right. Unk used to tell me that I cannot control what the others do to me, only how I respond. But it is hard."

"However, you haven't done anything wrong."

"It is just that being the object of the attacks, the nasty phone calls, the trespassing, the spying. The energy that lands on your feet and shocks you with an electric bolt being controlled and aimed at you from a distance, while someone squeezes your left arm as if with hands of iron, the same every day. Who are these people? Do they understand others have rights, not just themselves? One night, it must have been three or four in the morning, after being awoken by the old owner of the counseling agency, yelling over me and attempting to get under my blankets with the wireless stuff touching my buttocks; after I had to move three times around the house fleeing from the brute, I was falling into a daze from lack of sleep. This was going on for months, the virtual intrusion. I bought a noise machine and turned it on at night. That helped with the spies, pretending to do it under my window. But with the quantum physics leptons, this doesn't work. I'm beginning to worry about how I will respond when I am truly exhausted, and they don't let me sleep. That night I'm telling you about, I found myself with a hammer in my hand going toward the door. But I thought of Unk. That stopped me from destroying those silly cars from which they—"

"I worry also. And don't expect the law-and-order headquarters to help you. If there ain't a body and x grams of cocaine or a video more explicit than the ones you have, there ain't no crime."

"How can you work there? I mean I know, but …"

"I wonder the same sometimes. But probably I can do some good. That belief keeps me going." Rafi Salcedo is very good at what he does for a living. He does not lose his professionalism ever, not even when he is being the best of friends.

"Yes, you are right. Unk used to say that we artists are a corrective in a society that suppresses true emotion, thoughts that may be disruptive. You are that corrective force in your field."

"Gracias! That … That is a great compliment. And, since you understand, let me tell you how I became a cop."

———————————

(Renata wished she dared to tell Rafi Salcedo everything. But she doesn't. Not yet. But she rehearses dutifully how she would tell, something like what follows here, with the right pauses and emotions… *In desperation, with the Old Goat hurting my head with the electric long-distance pointers he uses to find my whereabouts, and then blocking both ears, I improvise, lashing back at the stupid brute. I laugh at the family that pushes AnnaLynn, the mother, to masturbate near their electronic gadget so the victim may hear her. Then I make a phone call where I know they will ask me for personal information, and I say I cannot give it to them because my phone is bugged, spied on.*

The Monster gasps so we all can hear I'm telling the truth but stays to listen more. Nobody has offered help tracking these bugged calls. I cannot make a private call or give financial or personal information. It is not important. As the chief of police said to the mayor, nobody is going to get killed here.)

SEVEN

IT, THE THING

They celebrate that the police are gone. They beep to one another and detonate a few firecrackers. Their lives are back to normal. If indeed the city is taking over the defense of justice, my defense, they will see what they'll do then. Nothing much. Step back. Hide. Lie as usual. Turn against one another if the investigation digs deep.

The thing, It, The Monster, starts appearing again in my room in the early hours, around four in the morning, cautiously feeling me up around the body, and then with a rough movement pushes my head, attacking the eye. Can this truly harm the physical body, or is its function limited to inconveniencing the emotions, the peace of the spirit, the natural need for resting time and aloneness?

But I move around and turn on the lights, and It stops. Same every day. Early morning, at the crack of dawn, the owner of the most famous counseling agency for poor people in Monument pretends to snore next to my mouth, every morning of every day. If I were to imagine terrible tortures, this would be one of them.

His truck, or a recording, rumbles, going nowhere around five thirty in the morning, followed by loud beeping from the son, who has his car parked as well. *Beep-beep-beep!* The inharmonious sounds are in honor of some of the ways my belly pain is relieved. Whether I am having any difficulties that day or not. This is eternal disharmony.

The Monster's own car resonates brutally, so loud and horrible that I wonder why the rest of the street puts up with this torture nightly. But I am learning about gang abusers: their cowardliness does not allow them to speak up for themselves. Both cars rumble, or a battery does, playing the offensive noises at two in the morning, ten minutes earlier, whenever, using oil and electricity to abuse, for the fun of it. The counseling-place owner and the future politician for the disenfranchised enjoy their power often, after computer games, harassing phone calls from unregistered and stolen numbers, and abundant grill parties in the yard. They have made it!

I look outside of my front door; they stop the noises instantly. They see me at all time. Two long and loud beeps are heard when the son leaves around nine, beeping as he reaches the top of the hill, as if he's the one to have the last laugh.

These are the people—Soto Sr. and AnnaLynn—who one day in that long-ago, irrecuperable past, fenced off by an injustice of the heart, falsely prayed with me for the health of the neighborhood, something they did, they explained, every day.

On Monday afternoon, until evening, I turn on the fan, so I don't hear their insults while working on my paintings. There is a growing pain installed in my belly, but much less swelling, a little gas. I am doing well with a very limited diet and a supplement to calm and replenish flora, but I can't live this way. That's what they wish for me: that I won't be able to live. My supper is a dish of boiled pumpkin/calabaza with an egg. I have forgotten how to breathe calmly, for fear they will punish me for that as well. I eat too quickly, disorganized and afraid.

I go to bed, watch a movie, and turn off the computer. And then, when silence reigns, after twelve midnight, Little Runt Emmett gets his big wish actualized by my back window. To come this close, he must trespass into number twenty-one, which he does, just to fart under my window. It must give him pleasure to do this every evening. A reason to live, it can be that simple.

This morning, around seven thirty, there is a continuous *beep-beep* down by the fence, the torn lullaby of the part-time mailman. His car is broken, but he beeps twice to comply with the gang. From a broken machine that disintegrates on his driveway, he can still milk out anger. Then he goes to my fence and kicks it hard four times. His duty done; he walks to the bus stop on his way to work.

The pleasure they get from their dissonances, a broken orchestra, is a sign of their poverty. They celebrate no holidays except those with names in the calendar, and then because they must. They have no music and no rituals. Except under my window, at night, when their voices reign all-powerful, when they can communicate to the rest of the street what they are doing to me and are happy to get away with it. Because they are together in this and proud of it. It's their patriotic right, to exclude or destroy the different.

Typing the handwritten memoirs by Unk in the middle of this jungle is my magic potion against dying in the heart. I love the rhythm of his sentences, the clarity of his message, the absence of grandiosity, the in-depth description of his education process---and the honesty with which he narrates his sexual experiences, so exotic in a way, so daring, but controlled also, as if the ordinary and the meaningless had no place in his days and nights. Where there is language, there is hope. At times, I think this is not the same country Unk lived in. So much has changed in the expectations of people's relationships and treatment of one another!

When awakened at three in the morning and cannot get back to sleep—or I am afraid to—I get up and go into the little attic room, close the door, and turn on Unk's old computer. Even if he was my uncle only through marriage to my biological aunt, he's still the closest spirit I've met. I recall times of joy, of communion, of learning how to look beyond petty harassment. I type until dawn, until my eyes cannot focus. I go to sleep then, balance restored, in the mood for a land where smiles may flower.

I feel electric shock around my mouth and upper body at two forty in the afternoon on February 25. It hurts the whole afternoon. Trying to rest, looking at my horoscope for signs of luck and deliverance from this mess, the Old Goat very carefully gets near my legs and aims for my vagina with something pointed. I move away in time, before he pushes it up with force. The filthy idiot!

Helplessness and exhaustion have begun to take a toll on me. I am sipping cosmic cranberry kombucha, and I cannot swallow, not even my natural saliva. I panic, but somehow, I remember to keep breathing through the nose. Somehow, I survive.

Images of these events parade in front of my eyes, wide open and unblinking, staring at the memory of the scenes I am living through. I look at the developing story, carry it in my mind, like a man dying of thirst in a desert would look at a photo of a waterfall. Remembering may save me; someone will believe me one day.

I imagine that I can carry out a plan to deceive the Old Goat and put him in jail. In this story I make up, I am in a motel room, opening a door. All is cheap and sort of clean-cheesy for budget adulterers. The man who has knocked on the door is Old Goat. He cannot wait. He has a lecherous smile on his monster face and lurches at me, but I know what to do and move to one side, so he ends up hugging the floor. He looks at me, angrily growling, while I laugh silently. A faceless friend comes out of the bathroom and says, "Who the hell are you, coming into my paid room? Police! Security!"

I run to the phone and say what the imaginary friend has just said, both of us playing our farce without much art but with plenty of hate for the fool, who sits on the floor in anger and yells at my friend that he was invited here first so "get the hell out!"

"Get the hell out!" yells back my anonymous friend. "Did you pay for anything?"

"You don't pay nothing if you're invited."

We laugh, and security arrives. The guard orders Soto Sr. to get up because he's being escorted out of the motel and into a police van.

"Call my son."

"I am not calling anyone. Just follow orders."

"My son will get you. He's a friend of the chief of police."

The guard motions us to move away from the scene, which we do while the Old Goat is helped to stand and then led down the corridor. I run down the stairs and arrive at the parking lot on time to see my abuser handcuffed and taken away, which I photograph with my tablet. I go into the police station and file a formal complaint.

I have told part of this fantasy to the therapist, but she says that doing it in real life could be dangerous. The man would probably agree to meet me at a motel, but he would come armed and with the son, and I would be arrested. Or the man would rape me and deny it.

I don't argue. Neither do I tell her that the fantasy included that she somehow came there with me and be a witness, nor that I don't have at this point any friends I could involve in anything so novelesque and crazy, not ever since Fred said no to coming here and be a witness. Rasheem wouldn't do it either, not if anyone is a friend of the chief. Out of the question.

Who says that trying something like this wouldn't put an end to the monster's rapist activity? At least I could prove I am telling the truth regarding the man's activities. I would seduce him and convince him to do this hotel thing while he is at one of his bodiless raids, which could be proof that he comes in here. Where else could we have spoken?

The fantasy starts fading, the way old black-and-white movies give up reproducing images, and show unruly lines and white spots on their way to breaking down. How can I expect---at a time when terror is portrayed, in widely accepted entertainment creations, in the shape of huge artificial animals and machines destroying aimlessly---that anyone is ready to listen to scary experiences that require of the listener compassion and imagination! To start seeing these experiences being done through old Native rituals, even from the unethical use of all these formulas and science talks that assure us that certain things like teleportation cannot happen in our lifetime. Opening the eyes to strange things that are not supposed to happen in our lifetime is something we must learn to do, urgently.

EIGHT

NO RELEASE FROM THE UNIVERSE

The universe answered my prayers and released me from its tyranny in the most unexpected way, I hear myself thinking. *And it had to be just so, this way, for the abusers to receive exactly what they deserved.*

I have been in the attic room, looking at the darkening sky and remembering how Unk loved the spot with the green-grey sky and bare branches of the oak tree stretched over the space that represented the infinite---seemed, from here, to be the infinite. Unk saw something here that calmed him. Every time was the same and new, the eternal return. This was beginning to be my spot as well, to make peace with the day retreating into a present memory, my consciousness.

I ask from Unk's spirit, who lives close to mine, to be released from The Monster's curse. Whatever lesson I must learn, whatever cosmic debt I must pay, I have done it. Or so I thought.

How can one imagine what goes on inside this barely schooled idiot, made to feel important by the bullying gang for his ugly actions!? In this story of nasty ghosts and a tribal public safety structure, what I am learning most about are evil deeds, supported or tolerated by a passive and biased environment, where any change demanded by the logic of decency was snarled at, persecuted. Things are as they are. And if you have the bad luck of being singled out to be the target of bullying, as Betty used to say to Unk and me, "Go and live in the woods!"

Fred has suggested more than once that I should take a long vacation to nowhere. This is what people without mission or destiny must think one should do.

As the police said, "No proof, can't do." Something must have gotten through the thick skull of the famous counselor, because he understands, correctly, that the police won't do anything to protect me. He is safe. The night of the day I reported him, AnnaLynn, and the upstart son, what did he do as soon as I turned off the light? The thump on the windowpane is heard, the air from whatever source blows against my nose, and his horrendous weight starts occupying my back's upper part. He knows the police won't stop him.

"How do you dare, stupid bum? Get out of here, or I'll call the cops."

The bodiless ghost disappears. There's no more weight, blown air, or pretended snoring for the moment. There is a kind of progress based on fear. Not really. Not fear. Just a maybe, a temporary what-if. Nothing will happen to him if that son with all the connections is right, and he doesn't have nothing to worry about. Do what you want. So, when I, the weirdo, read a book, the counselor can do something cute, like just one note of snoring. No more is necessary to dynamite the sense of security and privacy The son likes to hang by my couch when I watch a movie, laughs when a deadly event is happening "accidentally." He has plans for me. And when I'm asleep, the decision is to blow hard inside my nose once. I want to cultivate my cool and not give up. Are those two compatibles? More than you think, girl!

I sleep with the lamp on, in installments. It enters, announcing his stinking, invisible presence with the thump on the windowpane, and I yell at him, "What! You ain't with your mom? Dirty scoundrel, don't you dare to come in here, devil's bastard."

There's silence. The magnetic energy vanishes for now. I realize one of my victories is the restoration of silence. There are no more beeping orgies at midnight. There's less trespassing or spying under the window since the son himself, the promised politician, started being named to the police, moving away from the parent's house when the police came too close. But he's returning at chosen times, leaving his mark on the chronicles of pain. I know when he has returned. He lets me know. He does fireworks down by the parking lot with his GPS gadget, loud and odorless, at midnight. If the police show up, there is nobody there—no smell, no proof—and after that he shows up, as a ghost accompanied by some of the others, and walks toward me in my own garden. Only their steps and magnetic field reveal their presence.

"The good garden fairy protects me, unholy ghosts! Go away!"

They stop, a few times they have left after my words. It takes a little to clear the garden of their heavy aura, like that of men who murder.

The Monster comes back again, always. I am his life project. It is eleven twenty-seven in the evening. I keep awake just to be able to reject him at once. I finally have a plan. It took me too long to understand what a primitive, undeveloped brain inside a flabby body that exists moping around the house the whole day with nothing to do must think, if he is not rejected brutally at once---that he is irresistible, that you love him, that he is all powerful at least, and that when the son is raping a woman in virtual reality alongside him, they are the Invincible Sotos, counselors to the poor.

The Sotos, like the God that the poor women at the church have been told about, are all-powerful. And like the God the poor women have been told about, they can touch them and see them, but the women cannot reciprocate because they are just human and don't have those powers. Meditating on this real story, of poor women I have met---but can't save them, because their gentle souls were betrayed by the authority they trusted---is sobering. I am not that badly off.

It has been a busy time for all of us around here in December. The police visited many times, but we have not learned anything. I didn't hear any news from anyone around, so what happened to me next was very scary. If I peeled an apple for breakfast while standing up by the counter, hands presented themselves to sustain my behind, without being asked. I moved a few steps; they moved the same distance. I sat up at my desk, and excited breathing and a magnetic aura swept up and down my thigh, mostly up close to certain parts.

I stood up after rolling up a rug when cleaning, and I bumped against the "device" ---the optical color wires, visible at times, faintly. The Monster was present at any event in my former bedroom year around.

How to understand life now? Without privacy. I am stuck forever with a deranged idiot while vacuuming, using the toilet, reading at the library, lying in bed, waking up with The Thing doing his rape imitation in my bed from that other dimension. But how to talk about this? I wrap myself in a thick plastic sheet for the night. No-one wants to hear this. But plastic is all that protects me at night, all the help the universe has for me.

NINE

A PAULI-EXCLUSION PRINCIPLE-
GHOST MEETS RENATA

What color are you? Part of what makes you be must have roots in this world of shapes and light, since through your superior savoir-faire you have opened up my breathing channels, my soul. I sense pearls, a long, starry formation in the sky, from which your touch originates.

In the dark, sensing this exploration you do of my belly--- in a gesture ample as a wave and the innocence of beginnings---I imagine you appearing first into my life like a thin, silver chain dropping onto my hair, temples, neck, all the way down from infinity, playful, tentative, and dreaming of coming pleasures. Whatever you are, I do not want your touch to end.

I spy on myself, anticipating where you will awaken joy next, through what knowledge of nature and need: with what understanding of expectations. This night must be written in the Book of the Universe, this meeting of brother molecules that until now have been living like strangers.

Why choose me? Me, among all the living! To what end must I understand your visit? How to reciprocate? For you, I have attention, silence, the awareness of feeling, the memory of roses meditating under rain and dew---awakenings. What else can I present you with if I don't know what you are? What original consciousness sent you to look for me? With what part of myself could I welcome you? If you had a mouth, how would I kiss it? On my pillow, no mouth but mine. The skin of your hands, what would they say about your life? Here, there are no other hands but mine. And your eyes, what would they tell mine if I could find where they shine? Could I be angry at you, wish you banished?

I reflect on these questions; this is not a meeting of the minds, not even of feelings, just the awakening of pleasure in the body, jewels in my awareness like stars in the sky, pure joy—followed by emptiness, the coldness of the universe. There is something less than respectable in your presence. And that inhibits adequate thought and action.

We are not equals, and all in love should be. You do not salute me. You do not reveal a thing about your world. You don't tell me how I could find you in the morning or the day after tomorrow, even now, this moment. You touch me with your fingers of fog for some reason, but you don't love me.

I think all of this and much more that has departed unrecorded forever toward the discreet space around the stars, as the skillful ghost appears in my darkened room and, like a guest, joins me silently for intimacy's sake, as if he knows what our meeting, which he has just summoned without asking me, is all about. I am a witness. I keep breathing rhythmically, my eyes closed, because I don't know what silent gadget he may have, from where to see me, and I don't want to be disturbed by the unsettling thought.

There is no weight placed on me, virtually of course. A pleasant breeze leads the imagination to an idyllic landscape, inside which the ghost and I are casually sitting under a tree. He touches me softly when he wants to, as if gentleness were part of his nature. He has also shown anger at something he didn't like in my attitude. Those hands or fingers can approach the skin with authority, bring warmth to my breast, and play with the shape of flesh and spaces, like a musician on a keyboard. He knows where the feelings are waiting to be awakened. I consider how I would respond if my body's needs for affection were truly convinced that this could be love, that love expects a response, an affection of presence.

He reaches a bit lower than the belly, and at the same time, I sense a window has opened in this virtual labyrinth when the shape of a bed or a coverlet is revealed, not to my eyes but maybe to my skin, to my consciousness. There is no weight, a vibration, and his excited breathing hovers over me and then subsides, but he continues his caresses.

I keep my cool. Although my skin is very warm, I am attentive to his insistent, carefully explored caresses. I realize he doesn't have hands for me, just an invisible micro-location extension of his distant self. He doesn't hurry. I figure he can sense what I feel through some magnetic chart propped on his computer screen, or in his intuition.

I wonder what would happen to me, to my resolution of being only a witness, if the ghost would make his reason for being the searching of all my pleasure points through the night. But my resolution is like a rock, despite the warmth and happiness that travels my body, as if I were a child eating honey.

Stretching face down on my pillows, inviting sleep, I turn my back on the ghost. I need distance from this call from the sidereal side of passion. I am about to say "How lovely" aloud, but I am alone, and the man at the other end of this magical wire shows no compassion for the yearning for a companion I am revealing.

―――――――

No living man has figured out the rhythm of my pleasure's structure that well—my breast rising and my belly turning and falling like a wave—resembling a choreographed piece about the waters rehearsing their poems. My body is alone, without the volubility of kisses or the burden of hands holding another's. There are no promises, no remembered love poems spoken at the right moment to recover a happiness slinking away without the anchor of thought or the communion of beautiful language. There's just a touch, ephemeral, distant, and made entirely of engineered energy and consciousness.

This feeling of pleasure is real, starting, like all that exists, in the deep desire of the mind, in its effort to construct arguments against loneliness and despair.

TEN

IN THE NAME OF THE OPPRESSED

I am dancing in the kitchen Sunday morning. It's my ritual, my salvation! A rock version of *Hymn to Joy* is playing loudly, transforming my inner space into a sunny wave of beautiful sensations. I make coffee and look for cleaning rags, dancing down the corridor. I stop by the bathroom mirror, to start a few improvements when the song ends. But a fart, medium volume, booms from behind the bathroom curtain: his insult to me. The Monster has invaded the bathroom as well.

Vomitive. Disconcerting. Shattering.

I cannot think about It anymore. This Sunday I was looking forward to my rest and realize Rest itself is a thing of the past. Like privacy. Like being alone with one's body. The overweight counselor isn't going to church. It's his job, going to the back room behind the church building on Sundays, the day when the clients come. It's a good income for barely half a day of work. It must be why The Monster is allowed to do what he pleases, so as not to create problems in the business. He stays alone at home to do the barbaric actions he performs via magic teleportation or invisible sorcery. Who cares what it's called.

I am the audience and the target of a deranged counselor who never was convinced of the holy side of life. Now he has no incentive to go to church. Let Junior say a few important-sounding things to the old women who always come. It's a charade anyway. A way to make money. Who wants to be with the boring church people when he can be a peeping tom and enjoy sex tricks on himself with the vibrator; he likes being alone for that.

I clean despite the "presence", who giggles and touches my breasts from the shower. I spray the glass and look for the rag I had brought and cannot locate no matter where I look. It happens all the time with The Monster around, groping and looking, whatever he wants. Something happens to the brain. It's a kind of shock. You are alone cleaning, and someone you know has become invisible and grabs your genitals while you wipe the mirror. The inner road of our lives is so much more challenging, because no one takes pity on us when we are desperate for relief. We are hungry, we can go to the soup kitchen for apples and a smile. We have It in the house, and we are crazy.

A heavy breeze touches my face, again and again, as if a waste center had moved into my room. Smelly. There's a weight over my left leg and hip and arm, a heavy weight, and the unmistakable rush, the impatience of the counselor's sexual urge and smell. This time, there is a mechanical thing spinning where he seems to be. The Monster moans. He reaches out for my body and bangs against it, against my back, while all the time the mechanical spinning is heard very close, but the muted sound says the spinning thing is with The Monster's real body, inside some unnamable part. I move away, push him, insult him. Without result: he doesn't let me free.

His searching fog hands go to my backside, my buttocks. Feeling nauseated, I get up, but the hands are still on my butt. They come with me to wherever I am going. To the bathroom. I expel everything I've eaten. My response to terror. Don't we all have a bodily response to the invasion of our privacy, to this extreme challenge to one's integrity? This awareness of helplessness in the face of a total tyrant and a cowardly crowd must be what makes us look in awe at a Christ crucified, at a homeless beggar with a proud face. What would we do in their place?

My intestines rumble: they are in disarray, like my thoughts. The guy down the street plays the motorcycle recording that The Monster's son has made, to follow my toilet's water cistern. They all have that recording, play it often. If the mailman is not around, Emmett up the hill plays it. Shaming is a job of the whole community. I hear The Monster breathing hard while I am sitting on the toilet. He lowers his body/ energy, for giving a name to whatever is there invisibly suspended in the air, next to me, and his invisible hand touches my thighs and even my genitals. I have yelled at him, ran away, covered myself with blankets, refused any involvement with life. But The Brute waits, suspended in the air. Touches me. Pushes me. Hits me. Laughs. He has occupied my life.

Can he see me, in reality? I feel I want to vomit, but my body does not have any more food waste, only existential disgust. I move around the house aimlessly---but not *that* aimlessly. I am looking for the vacuum cleaner; finally, I find it and turn on the motor. If I could hike up the volume, I would, until the awareness of It searching for my backside around the room exploded. That must be how people relinquish their sanity, to avoid injustice and terror, to stand up as a mirror image of the stupid abuser; like Hannah Arendt described It, it is the "Banality of Evil."

Outside my window, I hear It yelling in his real body inside his dark den. As if by requesting freedom I had interrupted something he owns. Because he has the right to be here, which I don't, as he told the police.

I will sleep in the attic studio because I'm driven out of my living space by this strange invasion. It's good to have a refuge. And the whole afternoon, enjoying music, the chores completed, poems read, I get ready for sleep, always aware It could assault me again. I place by my side the Ghostbusters toy with the music, the anti-spy stick with the alarm, and the nightlamp. The Monster energy comes in darkness, in daytime as well. But he must think that he has me all to himself if I am asleep. I know he has just arrived. I know it, not only because of the thump on the window, but because of the air on my face. More than the face, the nose is getting the attack, the nostril that lets me breathe. The Old Goat knows something essential about how to harm. He knows about the one nostril bit, and the lungs' pressure points being in the left arm, and how to freeze an arm to a degree so low that it is no longer functional. There is a story here if anyone dares to dig it. But darkness of this kind is better left asleep.

I am being gassed with thick air up my nostrils, fetid air. I cannot breathe. I turn around, and the gagging breath is at my nostril's entrance soon again. I cover myself with the blanket, but that's a temporary solution. The anti-spy stick sounds an alarm, but he knows no one will come to my rescue, so he continues to blow the thick mess. I put a pillow over my face and leave a small space open, and I keep changing direction, keeping a tiny space between pillow and face, with the hope of fooling the *Hitler* goblin.

I check the time on my phone to break the monotony. It is twelve- twelve. I make it alive to one twenty-five. By two thirty-seven, when It has positioned himself on my back, heavy like a log, my bowels come undone again; they complain---and this he must hear because he starts peeing, wherever he is, I hear it. I stand up and call him everything that comes to mind: filthy, moron, stupid, empty-headed, disgraceful, dirty, son of a ... criminal, bastard.

Something must have gotten through because the air feels clean again. AnnaLynn must have pulled the cord. Or he passed out. Or someone killed him. But close to three in the morning, I am allowed to go to sleep.

The Thing comes back midmorning, using the same vocabulary for his one-sided conversation: blowing putrid air on the face, cuddling up his three hundred pounds on my leg, and leaving his stupid fog hands on my backside. But I have been free from three in the morning to eleven, eight hours of freedom from the abuser. Never forget that others don't have any respite. Endure with integrity. Imagine a way to freedom in the name of the oppressed.

I hide in the attic room, the little old bedroom for the maid, my refuge for poetry in less burdened days. I have brought my plastic shield and a blanket. When it's time for sleep, I will sneak in there. I have turned off the lamp to attract the privacy I lost, to confuse them until dawn, when I can leave the house unseen. They knock things off with their wireless rod. I always hope the light will keep them away, but not always. I turn it off, and in the dark, I organize the big plastic sheet to wrap it around my body the best I can, hoping they won't find me tonight.

I hear squeaking on the extra sheet of plastic in the other room, and I know they are looking for me around the house. I cover my head with a throw, breathing down into myself, the way I imagine the damned are forced to do their necessities in hell. Minutes pass, and I am not discovered. From the distance of dreams, I hear their wireless tool tapping a windowpane, a door.

I fall asleep, comfortable in my old green armchair, where I have been happy reading books. Suddenly, I sense the world trembling between my legs, coming up my belly. It's a guttural breathing I already know, the excitement of fingers on herself. It is AnnaLynn Soto again. The Old Goat must order her to perform the scene over and over; their brutality offers no variations.

How to convince the captain to investigate this Crime? He closes himself off to believing any of this is true. His sense of decency rejects that this debasement exists here, among us, in the lives of people the chief of police counts as his friends. It is one thirty-four in the morning. All services are closed since tomorrow is President's Day. There is no space where I am allowed to sleep.

ELEVEN

AND DREAMS, DREAMS ARE1

Rafi Salcedo climbs the stairs of his apartment building. He sees himself climbing the familiar steps. It makes sense to stay away from the elevator somehow at the time, while climbing and climbing the stairs, familiar every inch of it, he has seen all this before. The New Age brick wall was finished with bright-red and blue paint on pipes and railings, like a new school just unveiled in a made-over industrial building, which is what this old industrial building was converted, into a place for living, for dreaming, and for flying up the stairs dressed in his usual jogging clothes, heather-gray pants and navy-blue hoodie. All of it familiar.

Checking the numbers in his Fitbit tracker, he decides he feels so good that he could run like the best of angels for all of eternity, even for two more hours into the night up the stairs past his floor and up the stairs to heights he didn't know existed in this building—but somehow there they are.

He is running up-up-up, way beyond where he has ever been before. A space, a thought, or a reason for being that is not to be questioned. This present is the thing one is looking for, the thing of dreams: permeable, weightless, all-powerful, and infinite.

Climb, Rafi! Climb! Climb!

There's nothing here but joy of the present on this staircase of bliss, pure conscience of living in beauty, nothing to stop your way up-up-up, all familiar. Yes, this room is familiar too. It must be familiar. All here in this now is familiar; but then, what is familiar--

Rafi, observe!

Reality opens to you because you are aware; The Monster is visible to you.

You don't deny what you see.

The terrible reality of The Monster has been brought to you for a reason.

---

[1] Chapter title from "Life is a Dream" by Calderón

Rafi, observe!

What can be done but observe and accept, hard as it is? Don't accept, and you step back into what you are not--- the commonplace, the uninspired, the cowardly.

It's useless to deny The Monster is here.

You couldn't be yourself if you are so crummy that you tell yourself that you are not seeing that Monster, not seeing The Monster, that it's unreal.

The Monster Renata sees isn't real, although I see it now here in the room of my dreams, the terrible reality, the dream where Rafi channels Saint Peter and denies her dear one once and again and once more into eternity. Not only three times.

You err here, Rafi. You mess up forever in real time if you deny seeing The Monster. Rafi! Where are you? Where are you going, not with your body, I mean with your heart and mind? Whom are you turning into, telling yourself the ghost here is nothing to worry about? You don't like him and think him a puny little bully, but don't say he ain't real. Unfortunately, he is, in some type of demented dimension, a dishonorable presence from the world of shadows, fat and round in the belly with skinny ankles and feet and a dot for a head with a baseball cap like a punch doll in a circus, a distasteful apparition from the world of the undeveloped of the spirit.

Rafi, run!

But it's not to deny the existence of the moron counselor-turned-halfpenny magician trickster for old farmers with bad knees in need of amusement. You are not one to deny a ghost if you see the thing.

Run to pledge to be a witness for the universe. This sorry disgrace is also part of it all. You've seen the bully in one of his several horrendous forms, Rafi.

Others must discard manifestations that are uncomfortable and challenge them, but you can tolerate ambiguity and as many faces of evil as the universe sees fit to present to you.

It's an individual thing, you know, the power to see the nuances and depths of the world.

This is the kind of thinking Rafi Salcedo experiences in this sleep madness, whether it is possible--- not only to see oneself acting but thinking within the dream theme.

Isn't this too much to ask?

And he runs and runs and runs without a predictable staircase at this point of the unexplainable experience.

If you're terrified, you don't care for stairs. There isn't any safety net of the emotions/ intellect. You just run!

Fully invested in this mind-boggling vision and the ghost pursuing you within these rooms, running to escape analogic invisible bodies who reach out of the eternity of nowhere and grab your private parts because they want to.

The mother-fckr! yells Rafi Salcedo in his dream, wiggles, uncomfortable, not waking yet, giving whatever is needed for making sense of this mess. And if it means not waking up, let sleep come. Please let sleep come in, to resolve the nightmare in this dimension at least...

And he runs and runs and runs, passing through walls without a scratch and not even falling off when the stairway ends somewhere in the darkness---without the feeling of beauty, pleasure, and happiness he used to have in his real life, because now the brute counselor for the poor took all the joy away with his invisibility tricks.

But he is not one to be defeated, especially not in nightmares, not Rafi Salcedo, right in the middle of distress and terror. He defies everything; he defies his helplessness; he defies his anger; he defies the wall in this dream room. And he passes through it the way a quantum-reality particle would do, ending up being in two places at once, to the chagrin of this exact world of ours, which runs all that is supposed to happen through an adding machine.

And if what you feed the machine is not recognized as legit, guess what? Well! You are crazy! Rafi is somehow trapped within the unavoidable geometry of madness.

Others better than me have been locked up in Bellevue without a chance at parole, reasons Rafi Salcedo in his dream.

Rafi, who once thought he could be a famous writer, knows now, somehow, he could not deal with his sanity being doubted by the mainstream.

And run! Rafi, run!

This time, your panic is supported by research, for those dogs the fake counselor for the poor bought so Renata could not defend herself, not even complain, are also barking at you.

Those killer dogs follow you in the dream now that you sense somehow that the counselor for the poor has ripped your pants and is trying to get his little analogical thingy inside your behind.

In occasions like this, one does not need stairs, real or dreamt ones, to run away and fly or even fall flat, if that must happen, but you never calculate consequences---not if that's what you must do to save yourself. You go all the way down, falling helplessly to the bottom.

Out of breath with fear you are, for you think you are asleep, but the counselor for the poor in his ghost punch-doll outfit is hovering by your nose and pretending he's snoring. He'll do anything to debase you and then laugh with pleasure at your pain.

Yes, the bathroom!!! How could you miss that opportunity for privacy!

Run, Rafi, run! Close the door behind.

Lock it if the bully has not stolen your lock or key already. Push a chair or bucket against the door---but there is no use. Look at the door opening by itself. You hear the brute's breath.

What can you do, Rafi, to protect yourself against The Monster?

Call someone. Scream if you have access still to your own voice.

Here's a cell phone, your phone, Rafi.

Yes, that number will save you. Call Renata. Ring-ring. The third time, there is no ring: for the fake counselor to the poor has answered your call. Hear that terrible breathing.

Wake up, Rafi! Wake up. It is only a dream.

This is your bed and your floor. The door is closed. You are alone. But comforted by the memory of your friend Renata, who trusts you will help.

What are you going to do with this dream?

With what the dream may mean …

TWELVE

FEAR AS ANSWER

Fear, you have finally arrived! You enter their little minds, and this damned world I call the neighborhood gang association gets quiet, retreats. This space where we live, this hell, is quiet at last, on the surface. I taste peace in my mouth as if it were a holy nectar I had forgotten I earned. It comforts me. I can breathe without feeling that I should be ashamed of who I am---ashamed, not deserving this victory. Stay! Things cannot go on like before. I must rest. The neighbors must see the misery that their actions have caused. They all---the good people out there that make up this world---all must see, the respectable ones, those who form committees for urgent causes, even the forgotten. For now, I must hold on to the event that has given me a break. It's time to plan the steps to justice, what others call my vengeance.

Renata talked to herself this way, passionately, to drive away sadness. Wrapped on a blanket since she was awakened by Old Betty at two in the morning, she had figured out the action to take to move her defense forward. She had been on the kitchen rug, thinking.

And the answer was revealed: insist that the city's ordinances be enforced. Resist! If the police system was so undeveloped, the provisions of the democratic government were there to help. But really, Renata knew that for Betty and her neighborhood collaborators, ordinances meant nothing in themselves. What counted was if they were afraid of receiving a letter from City Hall. What counted here was fear.

Betty thought she was winning. That's why she went on edging the neighbors to continue their own harassing plans. Even if they were illegal. She didn't care, if they managed to drive Renata out.

Of course she wasn't afraid at this point. Why should she, when her son had tried a few years in the military, although he had to leave, something about psychological something. But that was important, her son and the military. She herself was important here, had lived in the street for a longer time than most. Everybody liked her. That Renata believed herself to be too smart, like better than the rest. Let her try going to the Council and proving to them with cameras and all that stuff that police ask for – let her prove that Betty did what she did. Waking Renata up any time. Every night.

The one whistle was the best. Standing in the middle of the night right in direct line to her window, fingers inside her mouth. And whistled. Emmett taught her that one. Sometimes she had to go down the street because Renata moved to another room. Betty was happy if Renata didn't sleep that night. Emmett treated her to a cold glass of beer. The whistle, and the mourning dove are the cleverer strategies, you know. She used to do the rocking chair number. As soon as Renata's light went off, Betty started rocking the chair. No stopping. She had already placed it in the right spot so it would feel as if the train were rolling over Renata's head. Didn't stop until she, Betty, wanted to sleep. But first she made sure Renata's light was on, reading maybe. Sometimes there were bets to see how long the street gang kept her awake.

Renata couldn't prove any of this.

———————

The break could come, although government things moved slowly. Not justice, but at least a tool to start applying for it in a parliamentary manner, in contrast to the gang culture that had camped in this stretch of the street. That's what Renata wished. The River Guard Institute worker who moved in next door gave Renata the opportunity. She had contacted him while raking her leaves. She invited him to coffee, and he gave her his email. Yes, they would be in touch, collaborating in the upkeep of their neighboring yards. Renata also said he should know about the new culture overtaking the street for his own protection. About four people had lost that home already because they got involved with Betty and Emmett.

"And she warned him!" exclaimed the assistant to the mayor, looking at the possibilities of a formal complaint based on the violation of city ordinances, with consequences.

It would have been the beginning of light and resolution, had this assistant not been so uninformed and thwarted by his own misguided prejudices. He then asked Renata, "What do you do to them? What's the problem?"

And what could Renata say except she didn't know? That she had asked, and her late uncle had gone and asked as well?

"There ain't no problem," responded Betty when Uncle Unk had gone up to see whether they could resolve whatever it was. "Just that I wish I had some schooling to make twenty dollars an hour."

So apart from the facts she had written in the complaint against the new neighbor--- another one in the long list of Betty's victims--- one more among the people anxious to fit in strange surroundings, hurting from their own unresolved burdens, ripe to be ensnared by the bully gang---there was the letter to Betty and Emmett, which they had refused to receive, certified and all as the letter was. As if not accepting it would erase their responsibility, to get them off the hook. The gang had to act united. They knew all was true but didn't want to see it in writing. No one was to open those letters.

It burned, while they held the envelope in their hands. They knew, because this was the second one for them. The first one they had read and knew it hit the nail on the head. Nobody confirmed anything, nor refuted something else. This silence was the worst.

They just wanted to drive her out, to crush a thing in themselves that had originated someplace else but was clamoring still for resolution. The anger they had inside needed this, to exclude somebody with the violence of the heart. They themselves fought for years, every afternoon sometimes. And nothing was resolved. Now there was a victim they would defeat. Betty and the others, trapped in their own internal poverty, gloated in advance with the celebration of that victory.

The assistant to the mayor didn't believe Renata. He didn't have to listen to this shit. This wasn't in his job description. He gave her a suspicion-inspired side glance and grinned with contempt. The secretary did too. He left the room without a word.

Uncivility must be a sign of the times, and I am behind again, thought Renata, contemplating the indifference of those taking spaces of power.

But incompetent and unlearned as this town hall was, Renata was not completely displeased. She had studied the ordinances and would pull from that thread to see where the gang ended up after she showed the world what happened to good people living in their own town, unprotected from the violence of organized bully persecution. Who would believe her? That's their strength. They count on the forgetfulness, lack of faith of the ignorant, and the prejudice of the elite.

Last week, the postman had called everyone to leave their chairs outdoors and make themselves absent. Action named in the Pyramid of Hate; discrimination when we deny equality of treatment. Because Renata had walked onto her own porch, she had to be made to feel unwanted. It's a violation of 31-51q in General Statute, Violation of Civil Rights, shunning as a way of torturing. And where there was a strategy, there was a commitment. A life built around a way of doing things and relating to others, creating an atmosphere of terror around those who do not join.

The predecessor in renting that house next to Betty's had done the same, led by the younger of her two sons, no older than twenty-two. All followed the gang's proposed behavior, no matter what their lot in life was: the young son's mother, a college librarian; Betty and Emmett, parents to someone who wanted to join the military; and the mailman, a veteran from the Desert Storm war. Nobody questioned the law of the gang. All of them were lost in a silent world without conscience.

THIRTEEN

EXORCISM

That night, I would expel this devil by the exorcism of song, for good. Desperation drove me to the belief that I could do so. I knew in my heart it would work. Not a helpless girl anymore, frozen under the menace of the abuser. I had a plan, strengthened by praying with the Jehovah's Witnesses who used to come to my door on Thursdays. They were sure that if I asked help from the divine, my situation would be resolved. I sensed that It didn't like us getting religion, prayers, and friendship for free in front of his window.

So as the two JWs and I were saying goodbye one of those days, now gone forever, a terrible fart fell from above in our midst, dynamiting our goodwill. The other two looked at me disgusted, horrified. The leader glanced around because she guessed correctly that it came from behind her, but no trees were there. The other zeroed her gaze on the socks I was wearing, of different colors. I saw it in her expression, unacceptable. But I had to think before I said anything, and not in the street. The Monster's miscalculation would come in handy, even if just to lead the authorities to understand his many filthy actions.

In the evening, I prepared the definitive trap for the fake counselor. Near the front window, so he could hear it from his black den with blinds from where he spied, I installed my laptop playing a three-hour version of Psalm 91 for protection from enemies.

I will say of the Lord,
He is my fortress,
My God, in whom I trust.

Surely, he will save you
From the fowler's snare
And from the deadly pestilence.

I went out to see if it could be heard outside, and yes, the soft, melodious voices of the male singer and a three-women chorus gave the outside of my house, with one window lighted, an aura of peace. Just then, something caught my eye. A huge light shone over It's door, and someone was covering it up, bringing it down somehow, hurriedly. A beam, the Randomness Beacon, shone in the direction of my attic window, the place through which It came as a bodiless ghost every night after stamping a signature thump on the glass.

In my investigations, so my description of these extraordinary happenings sounded as scientific as I could make them, I learned of a micro-location device that worked with a beam and a Bluetooth account, reaching sound and magnetic energy about one hundred feet from the source. So that was it! He was trying to hide his machine from me! The huge light was once in Hubber Dixon's attic. The night I was shivering with a fever, I was awakened by a strange bright light reflected on my ceiling, and soon after, there was the sensation of below-zero cold by my bed, like an invisible chunk of ice, which disappeared in seconds. These Hubber's transmutations of energy into visual and sensory manifestations were quite good but fleeting, like visions, like unworthy lives. For a few seconds, they could impress you. One night, I awoke with the figure of a man leaning over me, a sweater and a head, well-formed. It disappeared like the ice, like the warm embrace by my neck.

Empowered by the psalm companionship, I created another sleeping corner not far from the laptop, behind a door. I felt comforted and protected. Once, I got up to play it again, exactly as before. I had slept some time, finally. Probably It had given up, ashamed of his behavior, being a church faithful someplace on Sunday mornings. The sacred music I was playing gave him the chills and made him avert his eyes away from the light, figuratively speaking, since it was still night. A bit of dawn hit my eyes through the semi-opened door behind which I tried to hide from the virtual monster.

But the light wasn't all that had awakened me. A commotion over my left shoulder, over the upper part of my body. The Monster was shouting at me again, not with whole words, but imprecations and orders or wishes that were too ugly to translate from the language of the depraved. With his invisible wire fingers, he pushed my shoulder back and slashes the part of my chest under the collarbones, in a hurry, desperately. Maybe he was killing someone in his den. Who could imagine to what depths of degradation he had descended!

I got up from my pillows on the floor, and he slashed at me again. There was a tremendous force in the invisible energy that pushed. I ran to the bathroom, with diarrhea once more. The endless, literally out-of-nowhere harassment prevented me from retaining any food; it turned into bloating instantly. I was existing on less and less food to avoid gastric complications, with the corporal bullies and the ethereal ones using my pain to their advantage. Any sound of discomfort was cheered by the expectant leering attention of the abusers.

So many mornings did I wake up with It, member of a church and owner and counselor in body life, faking farts with his ghost mouth next to my ear! And silence I needed back in my life: disrespected, trampled on, spat at. Insulted silence. How to know I was alone? How to choose when to share my life? Should I keep the lights off while taking a shower? Where did the gentle silence that used to welcome me when I needed rest and healing go? The space reserved for the angels, invaded by the overweight fake, a debased Big Brother. And so, my own home expelled me.

Desperate, I crossed the street and knocked on Its door. It is eight in the morning, and he had been in his bodiless persona in my house the whole night. I heard him breathing behind the window with blinds, the same breathing that wakes me in the morning and in the wee hours, next to my mouth and my nose. Desperation inspired foolish things, but an action taken was a bid for justice, a statement with authority. The road to clarification—that twisted, suffering road, occupied by the enemy and its army of snakes and the cowardly—had in me a new traveler.

I could not breathe inside my own house; the air was oppressive. I could not understand the refusal to answer my questions and complaints, to face me. But that's the way of the abuser. Power was everything to him. The Monster despised me as a human being, and his own self-esteem rested on my suffering. He was not opening any door for me, just the contrary.

I was so afraid that I called the mayor on his cell phone. Unk had some friendship with this man, and his number was written on a paper taped under the phone jack. I tried to explain who was involved and what he was doing. Big mistake on my part. But how was I to know, that morning of Terror.

"I understand that this guy you're talking about is some kind of counselor or owner of something in Monument."

"The same."

"You think that guy would do anything like that?"

"I know he does."

"And why?"

"I do not know. Ask him. I think there is some imbalance here, something not right."

"Yeah, I see. That's correct, not right. Call Safe Futures. Here is the number."

I took down the Safe Futures number and told the mayor that I was also going to the library to research an article on how state police cracked down on a guy who had infiltrated a home with a camera and was spying on the residents. This could help. This experience could be used to investigate what was happening in my street. I did not imagine that the mayor had no intention of helping me get in touch with that well-informed branch of public safety, that the phrase "not right" was said in relation to me, not the abuser.

As I was talking to the mayor, I heard a cry that escaped someone, and something was turned off with shaky hands. I looked up toward the ceiling near the window, from where I would hear the noise against the windowpane signaling the wireless connection. The parabolic microphone listened in from that spot!

Quickly I got dressed, and took my laptop, a comb, and toothbrush, in case I found a space to pass the night. Locking the door behind me and running to the car felt like escaping a solitary castle, with a curse finally operating in the open and pursuing me. I couldn't use the landline phone in the house because It was listening. The Sotos had intervened it, hacking everything they could in the house.

From the nearby park, I spoke with Safe Futures, a very nice lady, but their services were just for domestic violence victims. I argued that neighbors could be counted as domestic abusers, especially since I lived alone. She understood, but there was nothing she could do. She told me to call 2-1-1. I did. This new polite lady suggested I call the police.

At the library, I found the article, and sent it to the secretary at the mayor's office. I would call later to see if he found out something. In the meantime, I could eat a sandwich and have coffee at the diner. Since when have I not slept? Not just a few hours after supper or an afternoon nap, but going to sleep at ten, eleven, or twelve and emerging refreshed from the world of dreams and silence, whenever I am ready for the new day. It had been months, a whole year. The dynamic was different now, but my body, stressed and secretly afraid, didn't know the difference between one torment and the next. One thing I had learned was not to be surprised about that "next." Trying to be cleverer than the abuser, as if I could avoid something essential of those attacks to claim my victory. Anticipating his move! Preparing mine! Being ready!

And I had been able to claim this sad victory sometimes, only sometimes, because I forgot to be on guard. I lived my life. They existed in front of the TV, behind the computer desk, waiting for the church thing on Sunday, or sitting on the back porch or behind the window, like Emmett and Betty, enduring the time off from routine chores. They were several people, with a lot of time and no spiritual project of their own, with no intention of giving up the pleasure that creating this inconvenience to my life obviously gave them. They waited for night to fall to come into my home in the form of magnetic hands of fog, remote-directed invisible wires, open microphones on the air, through the window, phantoms with designer-like costumes, such as the future elected official who strutted around my bedroom like a little invisible goblin shining with magic wands and golden halos---an enriched gang member imitating street urchins hiding behind a tree, waiting to trip the next runner that comes along. They were not out to kill, just to do harm.

Still waiting for the hour to call the mayor back, I remembered that the senator's office had a good lawyer who researched new laws or bills for community disputes. To see if there was a legal remedy to ease my distress, I called her. But the woman asked me to what source were they hooked up to access my house. I asked her how could I know?! She continued, saying they had to be connected to something. I told her that they are in their houses but close enough to be able to access my space wirelessly. I mentioned the possibility of the beam and Bluetooth idea to access spaces and people within a hundred-foot range, and the parabolic microphone.

She suppressed a giggle, and her voice became comically friendly. She also thought I was not making sense. She said she would look up resources for me and would call back. She never did. And the mayor was still in his meeting.

I wandered the streets of downtown, all of them distant now, unfeeling, elusive, almost startled at my presence there. So much had changed in my world! I was a stranger here. What I took for granted in my town—that I would be safe among neighbors, that authorities would be concerned for our security, and that an effort would be made to contact with public safety units that had made the decision to study virtual crime—was all an illusion. My body, a stiff cardboard-like separate entity, felt abandoned. There was not even a public service to give shelter to a person in my situation. For one building, you had to have crime-level trouble with your husband or wife. For another, you had to be homeless and sober. For the other services, nothing of what I was suffering from was real. The internet was teeming with gadgets, and in this town, nobody had ever heard of a parabolic listening device. I had started looking at the whole surreal panorama from a distance, as if it were happening to someone else.

And the library, my cathedral! I went to research the parabolic Peeping Tom caught by the FBI and the state police before I even had coffee. I had to eat something.

Half-fainting, I told the assistant, "Could I sit after breakfast in one of the rooms downstairs? There are five, all empty."

"Sorry, you have to be a nonprofit for that."

I sensed Tim, the assistant librarian, didn't really mean to put it that way, and if he had a chance to do the thing over again, he would have opened a room for me and even brought me coffee. But I was already on my way to the diner, with that half-pained, half-inanimate body of those who have been deprived of sleep long term by a merciless outside force.

It wasn't noon yet, and somehow the day had ended for me already since I could not go back home. Walking seemed out of the question: my shoulders felt heavy, and my eyes full of sand. It took forever from here to the corner. But I had to do something. I headed for the courthouse. Around the back steps, leading down to the parking lot and the current entrance to the different offices, I found a few bodies, isolated from one another, reclusive, self-centered, their dynamic annihilated. Did they feel as I did? Could they talk? Where would they go after now?

I went into the building and told the guards I was going to the clerk's office to ask a question, and they gave me directions after checking my bag. They glanced at one another, as if sensing a sorrow they should respect. I waited my turn at the clerk's office, and then I explained my situation to a middle-aged woman who didn't seem to be really listening.

"Wait here and someone will talk to you."

She disappeared, and soon a younger woman, a paraprofessional or law student, addressed me in a cold manner with a smile, "We cannot help. Call 2-1-1."

"But I already did."

"Call again."

She closed the glass window and disappeared into the shadows of a narrow corridor.

In the empty hallway, there was a bench, and I sat there, staring ahead. Time didn't seem to be involved, or rather it was just detained with me. Time and I were paralyzed. Time and I were stunned by evil. Time and I were without hope together. I had seen on that hallway, out of the corner of my eye, the sign for the state attorney's office, and I went back to try my luck there.

The man who came to see me, probably a lawyer working for the state, didn't seem to be in a hurry. He said something like the I had to report the event to the police. With their report and in accordance with the decisions made by the sergeant, they would see if there were a case for the court to act. I went back to the bench and called

2-1-1 again. The man who answered was not listening. You could tell when someone had put the phone on hold and came back when you stopped talking, to say this was a state hotline and I should go to a local agency.

I recalled there was a Catholic Charities office up the hill, by the church. Maybe I could just talk to someone. But it wasn't there; the building was occupied now by a professional training business. Dragging myself with some difficulty, I made it to the coffee space at the co-op, moving like a Frankenstein without a soul. I served myself some tea, paid, and sat alone in the middle of the space that made me ubiquitous in the preppy, alternative behavior that inspires every move of those who work there, mostly well-off volunteers.

I started calling some people that could maybe assist somehow. Every call was a hope being tried at the war front, instantly dynamited. The woman from the Jehovah's Witnesses, who could not come to the police to tell them what she heard, said she would pray for me and reminded me that the day after was our day for reading the Bible together. The manager at the homeless shelter also felt for me; she really did. We were sort of friends.

But Safe Futures is all she could think of, and they could not even offer me a chair to sit there, just because I was afraid of entering my home and finding It had his microphone still on. At night, he would hover over my bed, yelling and wanting to touch my private parts with his bodiless wired hands.

Somehow, in that magical eternity of thinking in despair, I came to a conclusion I could have never thought possible to even imagine. I would report It, The Monster, to the state attorney's office. Only after I started the process did I realize I was entering dangerous waters. The authorities, the system, did not want to know. But at that moment, it meant life itself. I finished my tea and breathed.

The process had started, and soon I was standing in the lobby of the police station. Behind the darkened window where the dispatcher was, I heard a woman's laughter again, probably one of those who had taken my declaration before. But this is not why I came.

I waited by the records window, where a young woman looked at me with a sorrowful face. Just six months ago, she had to tell me the supervisor had denied my request for records. Probably Officer Green or maybe the chief himself. Influenced by the future elected official, no doubt--- that disgusting ghost with magic wands that somehow worked for the police.

I asked her for a copy of the complaint I made on Sunday at seven in the morning.

She said she could not find it. I told her I was not leaving until she found it because I had been there at seven in the morning on Sunday. She found it, but she said that the only thing recorded was that I had been there, not the reason or against whom my complaint was directed. That might have been why the other one was not released, because it had the name and the information. It was just an idea I had to explain the mess. All this was highly irregular.

"I can write the name of the accused myself. It's Ferdinand Soto Sr."

Order came to the world with the word, as it should be. The dispatcher behind the darkened window stopped giggling, and the young woman at Records sobered up and gave me the copy I had asked for. I paid her one dollar, as requested. My phone rang...

"I am Marta from the city's Human Services. The mayor asked me to contact you."

"Oh, thank you so much for calling! I am so frightened!"

Frightened and exhausted I was, but I was also putting on a show for the incompetent and corrupt authorities. They were listening. I saw a glimpse of pity, of understanding, in the eyes of the young woman at Records. I felt she knew the Sotos and so understood the essence of what I was going through. If she could only speak, I sensed she was saying with her eyes. But she was afraid as well for a different reason. Frighten and divide.

"I would like to see you the day after tomorrow, in the morning. How is that?"

This is fantastic! I was so thankful the Human Services worker had called! I could return home after all! I planned on bringing the complaint against It to the courthouse; plus, the mayor and the social services were looking after my spiritual well-being! We were on the right road to figure out how to get assistance for all in need, not just for those content with a pill and sleep.

I left the police station a new woman. I knew exactly what to do, and I entered my house with the understanding that evil would not have its way with me, with us, the forces of light, like in that story about the Witch Cunégonde and the holy rabbi that Unk used to read me at night.

The Jehovah's Witness contact called me because she wanted to come the next day, Wednesday, to have our prayer meeting, but I told her we should not meet in my house again, not until The Monster's situation has been investigated and she and her colleagues were not in danger of being mistreated again. She understood.

As far as she was concerned, I was to provide all the evidence of It's abominable harassment. What she witnessed was between her and her God. She wanted no trouble. But I was in a good mood and promised to invite them to coffee at DD.

With whatever brain I had left after the ordeal and the nightly interrupted sleep,

I started writing the complaint for the courthouse. I decided that minimizing the description of the gross touching of unnamable parts by the ghost hand of the fat business owner would be to my advantage, because not everyone has had the strange bad luck of meeting such an avant-garde rapist. And it would be, for those without imagination or virtual reality exposure, unbelievable. But the spirit of the thing was in what I wrote, concentrated on his use of the parabolic microphone to intrude in my home aurally. It was more accessible for small-town cops, earthlier.

The rest represented the disgusting, maddening nightly abuse, the bodiless hands getting into my bed and touching my body, the pushing of my shoulders back to dominate me, and the squeezing of my left arm to harm my lungs, plus the nose plugging. We would hear from the bully himself when the judge summoned him.

Leaving the house that next morning was such a joyful thing! I had conquered despair and lack of hope! The nightly ghost abuse would be a thing of the past soon, and with that victory, the other jerks would fall into place. In a clean folder, I had my complaint, neatly typed; the sheets from the police that said I had been at the station, although it didn't specify for what; and a copy of the email I sent to It regarding the fart with which he greeted the Jehovah's Witnesses standing on my front porch, turning the volume up in a huge way with his parabolic spying microphone.

I made photocopies at the library, and smiling brightly, I returned to the state attorney's local office, less than twenty-four hours after they sent me away empty-handed and brokenhearted.

I said "of course" because I had no trust left, but that morning I was innocent, clean, inventive, hopeful, and sure that the pursuit of happiness mentioned in the Declaration of Independence was my true path. I went into that office and handed the no-emotion woman my folder like a bunch of fresh roses, and waited, but not for long. She came back unsettled, so deeply unsettled! Her chubby hands were like those of children who had stolen and did not want to give it back or acknowledge it. That's how I received my folder, her hands grabbing my papers as if they were hers and I had no right to even look at them.

"We told you yesterday this is not the place. Go to the police."

"But I did!"

"There was no decision made by the sergeant." The woman looked away from me as she said this.

"But I did my part."

"Sorry."

A glass door closing on your face was no argument; power wasn't concerned with how you felt. However, I knew what to do next. That's all one had, today. I walked down to the police station. Nobody received me, but at least the dispatcher behind the curtain didn't laugh. I stood by the Records window, and nobody noticed. Waiting was my strength. They could not deny that, these outdated employees. Finally, dragging himself as if he didn't want to do what he was doing, a young black policeman got up from his chair in Records and faced me.

"Anything I can do?"

"Yes. Please give this to a sergeant."

From a flat emotion with emanating coldness you could freeze on, he gave me a look of contempt. His lame hand took the folder. I reached out to make sure no paper was falling off, but he had the stuff.

"All right."

"Please give it to the sergeant right away."

He opened the folder and glanced. He woke up as if hit by cold water. His hands, fluttering butterflies, could not stop turning those pages and looking at the name written on them. The round moon of his eyes rested on me for a second, lovingly and grateful.

"Please, to the sergeant! It is urgent!"

He nodded excitedly, like a boy receiving a long-awaited present, and disappeared.

Out in the street, I felt whole, satisfied. I called the Jehovah's Witness contact and told her I was on my way to DD. This woman was not truly interested in learning what I had just done because she felt guilty and would not do anything about it. She knew something that could help me, but she was afraid of being involved. The other one, older and wiser, laughed as we drank coffee and sampled cut pieces of different doughnuts.

"Ha-ha-ha! You reported Soto, the old goat! He had it coming. But I don't want to be the one who does it. Good for you!"

Her younger companion smiled on the sly, without really saying anything other than we had to read the Bible, and looked at our inspirational videos where there was music for all ages. I welcomed their company, despite the narrowness of their spiritual proposals. It would have been much lonelier without them. We read a psalm, prayed, and hugged in the parking lot. The old woman understood; the other didn't want to---that there are times when we need to have our sorrow validated for itself, not in a vague sense of generosity toward the many general injustices. That was the last time I saw them. They knew it would be.

That I was crazy to ask for the head of the ghetto owner was communicated to me in the subliminal way things are spoken in the underworld. When I arrived home after the Bible doughnut party, a somber younger man opened Soto's front door and stood there, staring at me menacingly. It could have been the son or someone resembling him, I could not tell. I parked my car and stared back, after which it seemed to me, he backed down somewhat, got into an expensive SUV-type car with tinted glass, and drove away. In the afternoon, when I went to the shelter's chorus practice, a similar van followed me.

And that night, when I turned off my reading lamp, looking forward to a well-earned night of sleep, I heard the announcing clue, a thump on the window glass of the new room where I tried to rest, always changing places to fool him. The Monster was able to locate my body in light or darkness. A GPS-like device or program did that for him. This was before they took magnetic samples of my thorax and electric signals of my legs. Terror is a sidereal state or condition. Nobody can reach you and help.

Aloneness, a term that belonged there--- but remoteness, isolation, reclusion in nowhere, and without walls to protect, said more closely how it felt like to be at the mercy of a virtual-reality monster at eleven, one, four, or six in the morning, sometimes appearing at random stretches, others constantly mincing your body like a deranged butcher with the assistance of his fingers of fog and wire, invisible, into the morning lights, at which time The Monster's mouth would pretend to snore next to my face when I awoke from my short sleep.

Later, the microphone would be turned on, when my cell phone rang, and The Monster would participate in the communication with loud farting, I asked people to text rather than having them go through this disrespect.

That first night of the day after reporting It, he visited me in a rage, going straight for my throat. I didn't know whether any damage could be done with fingers of air and evil, invisible but with a metallic edge, so the pain I felt was magnified by fear, by the unknown. I moved away and covered my head with the blanket and waited for his anger to wear out and leave. But he didn't leave. He raged over my body, frozen by anguish, listening terrified to the brutal roar of a voice that sounded out without words, like in a pre-human state, while hitting my shoulders, trying to get me do something I didn't understand, nor would I ever consent to.

One thing I realized that night, when the worst of nightmares took shape in this life in which what was real had a name as proof, was the fact that part of him was so primitive as to prevent him from being able to communicate in a situation requiring logic. This could explain his failure to answer the door when I called, or the email requesting an explanation. His brain was undeveloped. But what about the family, helping him while he did this? AnnaLynn, the mean wife, and the son who had been a student once and got into politics as a means of rising in the world of the temporarily powerful. He would rather be the oppressor, period.

The morning It so brutally assaulted me, I showed up at the senior center, where two offices for Human Services are located. I sat on a bench waiting for someone to show up looking for me. Because I asked at the front desk for someone from Human Services, and the receptionist didn't know who I could be looking for, to call the number I had. I did; nobody answered. A woman, maybe in her late thirties, kept going by, asking whether I needed help and so on. Then suddenly she realized I was the person she was looking for.

"I didn't think the person could be you," she said when we were in her office.

"Why not?"

"Well, I expected someone …"

"Aged, sick."

"Something like that. Well, what's the problem?"

"A long-term harassment, which is getting worse. The police do nothing to help."

"Do you have cameras?"

"I do. But since the bullies are the neighbors, they know how to avoid them. Besides, there is a microphone in my home, installed wirelessly by one of them, and another with a camera. This is virtual intrusion."

"How do you know they are the neighbors?"

"Because I hear them. Sometimes I see them. Unfortunately, they are several, and I am one."

"I am sympathetic, believe me. We have heard a lot of stories about how women who live alone are harassed. Frightening."

Marta asked a few questions about whether I had family, friends, or anyone who could help.

"Unk died; he was my family. But I have a friend who told me I could spend the night in a spare bedroom he has. He lives nearby."

"That's great!"

"But it won't resolve the situation. And the bullies would have achieved part of what they want. They want me to leave."

She seemed torn between believing me or siding with the guy who sent me here, the mayor, who knew my uncle and maybe resents him. I remembered Unk telling me that in his conversations with the man now presiding over our town, the first elected mayor, he had mentioned that the proposed change in government structure was unwise because a person hungry for power and supported by his party didn't necessarily know how to manage a modern city. He would most likely behave as an amateur, and we needed a professional. This was the mayor's revenge on Unk. A part of him was aware that he didn't know how to be at the level of the circumstances.

"Did you try to resolve the issues?"

"Continuously. Alone and with Unk. We formed a neighborhood association, asked what the issue was, and invited them to come to meetings. Now that I am alone and there are new neighbors, everybody can be turned against me on the grounds that I am different, that I have an accent. It is the exclusion of the different. One of them recently shouted at me to leave because I am invisible to them, a nobody. Fascist speech."

"Was it always like this?"

"No. The population has changed, in its majority. But the original bullies remain. It is so easy now to create a gang mentality! Someone explained to me that these new neighbors are just getting out of their system the rage accumulated at menial jobs that they don't enjoy. Suddenly, they can pretend to be the boss and lash out at someone. I believe there is something else involved. A sense of belonging, which they don't normally have. A righteousness that empowers them. They are fighting for the unity of their country, against the foreign, the different. It is not like we don't agree on how to do something. They don't speak. They kick my fence, growl, make calls from stolen numbers, and hang up or leave a message with a group of people saying blah-blah-blah and laughing in the background. They throw trash on my lawn, place their dogs across from my house, and demand they bark. They are what the philosopher said we humans would become if we do not have music and kindness in our lives, vicious automata of self-will. That's what these neighbors are."

Marta looks at me and smiles. She hesitates before she says, "Well, I can tell you this much: you are not crazy."

"That's what the mayor said?"

"Yes. He called my supervisor, instructing her to interview you."

She says I should find something to do, like come to the senior center to help wrap presents for Christmas.

"But I am too busy already. I have created a chorus at the homeless center, where I oversee everything, including getting funding to pay the singing instructors. Apart from organizing Unk's papers and typing his memoirs for publication, I work full time every day."

Marta made comments, more or less disconnected from each other. Maybe she really didn't understand this life of the artist, while taking down my insurance information. She believed that I was very sensitive, and that was part of it. But the situation existed independently of my personality, I told her. I had a hunch the system was uncomfortable with this because the criminals were not the usual suspects. No blacks were involved. Nobody was on welfare or homeless. Most of them were voters on the mayor's party list. The so-called counselor's son, who had jobs in stores and a gig at the police station listening to the stories of drunk drivers on probation, was being groomed to be some kind of elected official because he would bring in lots of votes. But I didn't tell her any of this. She was an employee doing her job.

"I am going to give you an appointment with a counselor, just so you have someone to talk to, to see how it's going."

But I never heard from her again or the mayor or the sergeant. They were not interested in how I was doing, just in seeing whether they had proof against me.

FOURTEEN

MEAN STREETS

Dolor duerme despierto
aquí donde yacemos
contemplando la nada

En las calles abandonadas
se nos exige silencio

Rafi lifted his gaze to the window near the ceiling in headquarters, the sky beyond just imagined, and exhaled, deep in thought. What a great heart those concise lines suggested! Would they carry the same heartbreaking meaning in translation?

PAIN sleeps awake here where we lay / Contemplating the void.
In the abandoned streets, Silence is demanded of us.

Yes! The tremendous message was not concerned with the language of power but with the innocence of truth. This lonely poet was dead now, but his voice lived. That's why Sister Marisol collected notebooks and drawings among the people she helped at the CASA Soup Kitchen. She perceived the strength of poetry when standing up to loneliness. How else could one survive the extreme conditions of this existence? She was no scholar but could read and listen. To be a witness was the ultimate religious act, she said once. To accept responsibility. Sister Marisol would be remembered, yes, not essentially because she started the soup kitchen, but because she dared to be a witness, while most pretended not to see. Ever. No matter how corrupt the situation.

That's why she welcomed her reassignment to the border mission, away from this civilized hell. The excuse for taking her away was that she spoke both languages. With her gone, things were not the same. Without her, bullies took over like starving rats.

Poverty was not necessary; this he learned from Sister Marisol. It had nothing to do with money. Poverty was in the heart, in the actions dictated by the indifference of the social structure.

He had just learned that he was going to get his old job back. His happiness was dampened only by the realization that the surge in crime in *El barrio* was responsible for his going back to being an undercover cop. Whatever the reason, that's where he belonged, where he did his best work.

He made up his mind; the clothes were in the car. He wanted to be in *El barrio* now, again, not in his professional role, but as a private citizen. Out of habit, once his official shift was over, Officer Salcedo left headquarters and drove to the park behind the trash-collection facility, empty until dark, when hard-living lovers and pushers turned it into the place to be. Ah, the incompetent hand of the so-called alternatives protected this space for crime. It would be safe now, if the opposition group had allowed a partial sale to the River Guard, who would care for the space, keeping its ecological identity intact. Now it was run-down, trash everywhere, abandoned cars. Forgotten until election time.

Hiding behind a cluster of pine trees, Rafi brought his classy bum costume out of the trunk, as it should be, unwashed and crumpled, as if it had slept many nights in the gutter. He changed his appearance completely: messed-up hair, dirty matching nails, the rouge cheeks of the wino, and the clueless smile of the dropout.

"I don't know what's going on" was a valid explanation, a kind of triumph for the defeated who couldn't accept their present for what it was. Armed this way against being recognized, Rafi waited for darkness. He drove behind the toothpaste factory and left the car well-guarded by dumpsters, taking with him his yellow plastic bag with the hard half-donut inside.

Night in *El barrio* was home. He smiled, satisfied. He was only partially in disguise when remembering. Freedom meant feeling loved, finding the world familiar: a loud salsa suddenly approaching you from a running car and disappearing, your identity a shield against a heartless world, and the smell of frying *bacalaitos* escaping a window as a welcome ritual.

Rafi was happy. From the corner of Luis Car Repair Shop, he glimpsed, next to Saint Augustine's community hall, the last men in the soup kitchen line, and he was then transformed solid into his bum persona. He considered, just for a minute, going into the lunchroom, but thought better of it. He might have been recognized, so he thought he would just loiter around the line mixed with out-of-luck men and women, as if waiting for his turn to go in for charity supper and changing his mind at the last minute with some pretext, leaving with no explanation. The homeless don't need any.

"Me, me don't know. Ask director, no me."

The part-time janitor at the Caribbean Community Center had been drinking. Estiive didn't like speaking in English, except when tipsy. Then he tried explaining himself by requesting that you ask a person of authority, not him. He knew nothing. And that, for Rafi, was a clue. The part-time janitor could barely communicate in English, but he knew something important.

Rafi lingered, eyes half-closed and body swaying just enough to pretend he was high. Persevering, he was just two men away from the part-time janitor, closer and closer to the door he must not cross.

The man was speaking in Spanish now. *"Ahí hay algo, si quereh sabel la veldá."*

Yes, Rafi understood that, although the others didn't seem to care. They had heard it before. Nothing new. Something fishy was going on at the community center. It didn't have enough money (so they said) to pay for the janitor full time but would ask him to do extra, a bit more of this and that in sneaky ways. Charity was everyone's responsibility, he said, but it left him with nothing for groceries. Why did he bother working at all, if at the end of the day he was like a beggar, the last in the charity food line?

Rafi, the bum, was listening. Suddenly, he heard yelling directed at him! He opened his eyes to see what the commotion was, and there, not even three inches away from his own face, so close that he even smelled the pot breath and got spat at near the left eye, was Raheem, the restaurateur of spicy fries' fame, yelling at him.

"Eh, you, leave! Go back! Stinking bum! Learn English!"

But the direct stare by that unknown bum he was insulting froze the yeller, who left himself instead. The other food line-dwellers raised their eyebrows briefly, going back to their memories or snooping on bits of conversations. What was new? Anything? Yes, that yeller was black! Anyone had seen this regressive behavior before? Yes, they had seen it all. Only Rafi seemed shaken. It impressed him so much that he started drifting away from the present misery to his knowledge of literature, to be able to put his own pain in perspective. Had this happened before to anyone more important than he? He remembered the books read on the sly, those that were not supposed to be accepted literature, the canon, but that spoke to them kids in *El barrio.*

Harlem. It wasn't right to be ashamed of what one was. It was like hating Mama for the color she was and Papa for the color he wasn't.

"Piri Thomas, where are you now that we need you?"

Officer Rafi Salcedo, the bum, almost said it out loud, a cry of sorrow, of pity for what his city had become, for the silent sorrow that no-one wanted to acknowledge. But he caught himself just in time. So that nobody would be bothered by his pain.

Rafi was a professional, the best, even down these mean streets.

FIFTEEN

OCTOBER 21, 9:32 PM.

I just had one of the best laughs in a long time, ever. Of course, the owner of the people's counseling place in Monument visited me, like every night, especially now that he had been reported to the sergeant and they had absolved him. He came like a cat on iron paws, reminding me of the beautiful poem about the fog, twisted in ugliness. Then he lashed at me, yelled, and shook me, all the things he must have done to helpless women in real life, an inner violence actualized in this ghost world of fantasy and injustice that gave him the lowest kind of pleasure. He knew he won't be caught.

At about nine o'clock, I turned off the light, my hand near the button of the Ghostbusters music toy. I heard right away the thump on the window and then felt the mass of energy coming closer and closer, to make me afraid. I then heard the breathing of the ugly scoundrel and smelt him. He stank. It was then I turned the toy on. I heard the cry of surprise and fear, and It, The Monster, disappeared. The famous counselor was afraid of my plastic toy! If a genie had told me that laughing now would make me go insane, I would have laughed harder. That was how good it felt. What a great moment of triumph! But It, The Monster, tried to come back. I didn't wait that long and turned the silly thing on again. I waited for fascinating results. Probably I wouldn't be able to sleep but decided to lay down and meditated on this nightmare. I wanted to create a prayer against its triumph. Closed my eyes and responded with the toy strategy as soon as the abuser approached! Hesitating gives him (It) determination.

These hours were not memorable. There was no apocalyptic light and no huge revelation. Just the overweight bully coming back minute after minute, I did not know why, because I was awful to him. The mass of electron's warmth approached my body. I heard the sick man's breathing, and I turned on the ghost toy. He vanished then but came back. If I was asleep, he made noises, tapping the stove. Other times he tapped the windowpane. The bully wanted my attention. I had gone over to his house to ask him why, to order him to stop. But he won't face me. An abuser like those in legends---distant, intolerant, violent and monstruous, greedy, incommunicative---hiding behind his blinds and his façade of respectability. It didn't want to be unmasked. It wanted seedy power because I was powerless; my powerlessness gave him the real pleasure.

I didn't hear him this time farting on my face or reaching for my behind with his wireless fingers. He seemed to be waiting for something when I woke up. I turned my toy on. I went to sleep again and did not check the time. Again, it was a long night, a pivotal night. *Things won't be the same*, I thought to myself, *either because the monster has changed or because I have plans*. One of them would be to spray over his home's façade. *Jail the wireless abuser!*

Or something like that. But I moved on to a strategy that could be potentially more effective: a note to officials running for office in which the plea for help was on behalf of the criminal himself. I thought first that The Monster's name had to be there, but without a name it would be more effective in the long run because it put the focus on the need for help and safety, rather than on vengeance.

But I didn't do it. They would say they didn't have enough information to do anything, that it was not their district, that probably this was a joke from the other party, that this couldn't happen. Although I rejected the plan, being able to think of something had given me relief from despair. Hope was mine forever.

Since eight this evening, Soto's father had been fake-snoring when I fell asleep, making farting noises, following me around the house. They raged for revenge because I had told.

At about three in the morning, I was awakened by a body on top of me, the son, that future politician of my nightmare, touching his genitals, moaning. I turned away; he vanished. The father lay next to me at four thirty. I got up and came downstairs for coffee. I now imagined more clearly how many tragic roads started in a morning like this one.

In the living room, grabbing my left arm with great strength, The Monster tried to prevent my fleeing from his clutches. Pressure changed in the air, with electrical activity and eardrum piercing non-stop. One could pass out in these conditions.

I went to city hall in the morning, and it was quite peaceful in the afternoon and evening, as if they were afraid. How desperate one must be to count on fear as an ally!

SIXTEEN

STATE OF ALERT

"That's right. You report him to the police; he appears in your house in a second or whenever he wants, only that you don't see him."

AnnaLynn is speaking at Betty's, explaining the invisibility process. Renata could hear the bullies from her attic room and is in a state of alert about her immediate surroundings. The ostracism and the indiscriminate attacks, the chilling echo of their hate, is the background of her days. Typing Unk's memoirs, the songs' lyrics, and painting the old panels of wood recovered from forgetfulness in the basement---so many things provide stability to her present! The past sustains her life. Don't we all live, in some sense, in the past, in our memories? Photographs and names of people we connected with once but are now gone, live herein the heart, part of who we are and where we come from.

They are at Betty's porch. The first days of the year are unseasonably warm, and half of the gang has gathered for news and instructions. Did the *Aquelarre* gathering want her to hear any messages? Renata counts AnnaLynn; Betty; the special education daughter, Doreen; and Emmett. She doesn't hear whole sentences, at least not long ones, a story told in an impressionistic manner, in kicks and swearing.

"She gonna get it! Who do you say she told? The president?"

"My son say it's her for sure."

"Yeah! That's what she do! She tell! I'm gonna kill her!"

"Don't do nothing yet. My son an' his dad gonna fix her good. They track her wirelessly."

"But you can't hurt her that way … you mean online … I don't believe it …"

"You can't shoot her if that's what you mean, just bother-scare-piss off-touch, all that you can do. And leave her paralyzed with electric shock."

"Hope she go crazier than she's now with that stuff you say."

"Don't count on that. But we'll drive her out somehow. Just call and tell how your boys are doing kicking the bitch around."

"I'll drink to that."

Doreen will drink to that. Even without anything to celebrate, she will drink. Emmett wants her that way. Renata believes now what Unk used to say about the recurring family arguments. There was an untold story with many chapters. Betty exploded daily for any reason, practicing for when Emmett took off with one of his buddies and returned drunker than hell.

It was then that she called him Little Runt-Crap-Old Goat. She threatened with telling, "You ain't tellin' shit, you old fool! Who wanna hear this? It's your fault too."

Betty, Emmett, and their active collaborators, the Sotos, rule the street now. Nobody dares to oppose them. Now that the wireless attacks on Renata had started, some are afraid. Penny and Matt across the street are, just in case their house is wired as well. How do they know it isn't? Young Ferdinand Soto sure is handy with gadgets: he could hack old phone numbers not in service and make calls from them, as if someone else were harassing you. What couldn't he do with the dark, deep internet? It's scary just to think of it.

Renata knows what they are doing and had reported them to the police. No answer. But the chief had sort of given her a response through the local press. He had summoned a reporter, an acquaintance of Renata's, to rub in the insult, and showed, with ridiculous photos, some masks the police could use to intervene in dangerous domestic violence situations remotely, like from the next room, for the safety of the officers or to convince them not to be rude to one another, since this gadget was watching. The chief said they were going to train other districts so that people, like Renata, wouldn't go around saying they were not modern.

He has an idea that something is going on for sure and is letting it happen. Renata doesn't think that Ferdinand Jr. has shown the boss, the chief, exactly what he and his dad are doing. Probably the chief thought they are using a drone to spy inside the bathroom when Renata is taking a shower. He could do that too and get away with it. Easy. Nobody is gonna kill no one here.

Believing in the kind of things Renata is saying seem to be prohibited, as if they know Renata's words are true somehow, and yet they were not ready for that unavoidable truth, the disturbing thoughts that are demanded of you! Such awareness of the dark! Whatever it is, it strips one of all sense of being safe, taking away your self-assurance. Faced with Renata's story, one feels to be entering another dimension, a reality so dangerous that the floor falls under, and nothing ties you to the familiar any longer: abandoned, in despair, without rules. Nobody has openly said, "Don't believe the stuff." It is rather an ingrained taboo within the system. These kinds of things are not supposed to happen. The police controls the criminals. Science explains what can happen in the world.

"Has anyone checked this Renata woman for mental health issues?" The question pops somewhere else, not on the gang meeting porch. The gang knows what she is saying is true or something of the truth. But she shouldn't say. She's a nobody, an outsider. Whatever happens to her, she has it coming. AnnaLynn pushes the idea of Renata having told, repeating the same words over and over. And Renata is listening. *Told what? To whom?* She has told plenty to the mayor and the police, and the gang never came out in a horde then. They hid until the excitement died down. The thing must have gone public somehow, and that is a reason for lynching. Renata, watch out!

Could Rafi's town acquaintances have tried to do the damage? Good for them! She is sure she should not put any pressure on her friend, even indirectly. She shouldn't ask. Commenting on the gang's meeting could feel like suggesting he do something. Renata must trust the universe.

The first sign of trouble happens Saturday afternoon by the old desk in the dining room. Fog hands keep coming up her calves and thighs, trying to get under her buttocks, as Renata types from her uncle's manuscript. The pointed element of the invisible torture menagerie, the electric head, does the prodding, the listening, the uttering. In this way, a specific event in the invisible world could be executed, like farting from their world into your anus. Probably they allow the stinking counselor to snore symbolically by Renata's real mouth. Renata tries to explain all to herself in view of the experts' silence.

Renata could hear the old counselor breathing hard. But he is not alone. The prodding is happening by going fast up the legs to the genital area, with strength, as if operated by a young person, while the fog hands have settled on the shoulders, at both sides of the head, and push carefully forward, a little to one side and then the other, to control her. These are two men. When Renata stands up to shake the intruders, the fog hands act as if glued to her back, and while she is standing by the kitchen sink, she is pushed forward with strength. But she is ready for the attack and does not move an inch.

Would the counselor let her fall? Because it is he, the taller one with the bigger hands. He keeps blowing on her face, showing up in the bathroom and gasping wildly, as if with emotion, when Renata does her necessities, mumbling to himself from the other side, from the relentless hell house.

In the night, Old Goat is most hateful since he's not loved, but instead recognized for the monster he is and called coward for not daring to come in his real body self and risk the consequences of his disgraceful occupation, to torture a person who has not harmed him and do this as his mission in life, day and night. And when she is away from the house, he does this as well, tracking her with his GPS gadget, just to impose his despised presence and so prove his strength, even when he has been exorcised through prayers, identified as the spirit of evil, reported to the FBI. Even so, he returns at night with a new approach at domination: covering the woman's half-asleep body, outlining her slim frame with the suggestion of a tanning bed, heating it to the point that Renata smells the electricity burning, tightening the frame around her heart and up her skull. Then, The Monster places the heat on her genital area, but she turns around for protection, the same way she places arms around her breasts when the brute puts the pressure there, stupidly, like throwing a ton of cement over a flower you cannot kill. She can still move and reject the oppression. For how long will this struggle between good and evil last?

For as long as hope and gentleness can stand up to ugliness and violence.

Renata, your quest is sacred. Don't give up.

SEVENTEEN

THE RIGHT TO PROTEST

"Oh, Ah, Uh!"

The voice is right in front of me, a heartless playful pretense, when I bump into the monster in the middle of my former bedroom. There is something solid inside the visually empty air. The owner of the people's counseling place in Monument is getting cozy and fresh. One afternoon, after a long walk, I stretch out on the attic futon to rest before starting the usual session of typing Unk's manuscript when a voice on my pillow says, "With whom? He-he-he."

The creep! He asks me with whom I am making out while occupying himself—in virtual reality, astral traveling, or something unknown—my own bed!

Before I learned to yell at the monster, I was to suffer many moments of humiliation and impotence: waking up, in the hallway, in the kitchen, in the bathroom, trying to get some sleep in some corner of the house, at the library, and as a patient in the hospital. While sitting and waiting for medication, he tapped my head with his wires and felt my thigh the way he does, just to make sure it was me. But the night that turned the dynamic of the nightmare came at the end of the Christmas Day week, the night of Wednesday into Thursday.

I had come to watch a movie on the cushions of my former bedroom. I had lots of blankets and felt so warm there on the rug that, when the movie ended, I closed my eyes and turned off the light. The thump on the windowpane came right away. The owner's virtual body cozily snuggled itself against may back. I moved away. The Monster was not impatient by my refusal. He could wait, and soon he appeared, sort of standing by my right side, mumbling in that language of abuse that allows only one person to garble, looking down at me. I covered my head because the blowing into my nostrils had started, very close, relentlessly. I turned one way and another, with covers over my face and even with a pillow. The Thing found the angle for directing the fast, thick, smelly air into my nostrils.

Sitting up in a rage, I told the bastard to stop it. "Go to hell, son of the devil. I curse you!"

That sentence must have done something because It seemed to have departed instantly. It was well after two in the morning. I had been awakened how many times? My heart, so strong and faithful, raced, as if urging me to bring safety to our poor body. Where could I go in the middle of the night? Into my car? He would find me there. I realized how easy it would be to kill someone this way. The Monster was a killer in intent. He knew I was aware that attacking the ears was a sure way of making the targeted person lose balance. He had tried it, and I had fought it successfully. Now, it was the nose. Plugging it when one was asleep and unaware, with an intense dose of thick smelly air.

The lamp was on, and I prayed that between the light and my curses, plus the advanced hour, The Thing would forget about me for the rest of the night. I dozed. Sometimes I was semi-aware of a presence, but I could not wake up completely and face the sordidness of this present. So abandoned I felt that I wanted to sleep, as all consolation available to me. But suddenly I was fully awake. The lamp was on. It was still dark outside the window, and two voices tried to keep their exchange as inaudible as possible.

"Is that you again, Monster?"

Silence. I could hear the shock, shock because I knew, they were holding their breaths. Could I see them? Then I said something that would be essential. How did I know what to say?

"What happened? Your mama has not returned home yet? Is AnnaLynn with her?"

But AnnaLynn was there. She cried out, "Let's get out of here!"

And the machine was turned off, loudly and carelessly. In ten minutes, a car drove off in a hurry.

What degradation! To be so filthy that they would intrude in the middle of the night into the home of a lone person, someone who once asked them for help because she was being abused! Now they have joined the abusers in the most miserable of ways.

When I went at seven to put the trash out, the rest of the gang knew something had happened. I don't know whether they had learned any details from those who fled, but at least they imagined what it could be because they must have heard me yelling inside the house. I felt that Betty and Emmett were afraid of this virtual stuff. They had originated this sad saga. But their attack was simple: a bit of trespassing and kicking and much slander. It couldn't kill anyone and did maximum damage in all other areas.

They were silent with respect to the Soto ghost criminal nights. I could sense terror in their deep, long silence.

I knew, as soon as I understood AnnaLynn was involved deeper than expected, that I had to denounce them all. Would any of these reports bring me closer to deliverance? I put on a short dress skirt, brown leather shoes, and my best coat. When I showed up at the police station, the person behind the dark curtain didn't laugh. The policeman came out with a sheet attached to a board but no pen. When I told him I was too tired to talk because I had not slept, that I wanted to write it, he pointed at his breast. He was videotaping me.

Briefly, I described what had happened that night. I also said that I had denounced the situation before, that I believed they (the police) didn't care and wanted me to leave but I would fight this. The man sort of nodded. He looked bored or confused. He glanced at me with half-closed eyes from the great distance provided by indifference and mindlessness. He didn't ask questions or comment.

When I finished with the narrative, I said, "You didn't ask who I am denouncing."

He expressed something like shock. He nodded.

"Ferdinand Soto Sr., Mrs. AnnaLynn Soto, and Ferdinand Soto Jr."

He breathed in the information. My vindication had to be, for now, moments like this one, when I tell an inadequate authority that I need their protection, describe the crime, and name the criminal. Nobody protests; silence is a great communicator. What do I want out of this? Not to be like John, preaching in the desert, but to be a harbinger of the heart that will open us to dialogue, to civic responsibility, to justice. I want to be that. I want to believe.

I arrived home and sensed my street observing me expectantly. There are feelings in buildings, as in nature. Where had I been? They always wondered in fear when I dressed up and had a folder in my hand. The Sotos were not back, which was unusual, and it must be a sign. All had put out their one trash container, plus the recycling bin, except the Sotos, who left at five thirty this morning and were not back to put out their customary five bins for the trash truck, no recycling. There was a healing emptiness instead; let's put out gifts of neighborhood, hold hands, and plant hope instead of trash.

Making coffee without ghost arms holding my behind was happiness, so much that I answered the phone, a familiar number with a VOIP caller heading as a name, 580.0628. Maybe an investigator was telling me there was a conversation started and they were looking into the thing.

It was AnnaLynn, yelling "Renata!" She was not crying; just afraid people would know. She hung up.

I called back. She disconnected. It was unacceptable behavior. They always called, sometimes from a real phone number, but it was they who could say anything. I couldn't. The fact that she pronounced my name told me she had heard from the police. She never expected me to have the guts to do it. Now she knew I did, forever did. Now she knew how to pronounce my name.

The Monster came into my bed shortly after I turned off my nightlamp. This was the night following my police complaint. I got up and left the room where I hoped to find a refuge for the night. I looked outside the window to determine what was going on across the street. Several cars were parked there, as if someone were keeping him safe.

I went downstairs in the dark, and the corridor welcomed me with hands that grabbed my butt while fetid air hit my face. When I reached the cushions on the floor, his voice came from among them, "Ahhhhhh! Ohhhhhhhh! Uhhhhhhhh!"

I slept on the rocking chair, wrapped in the plastic sack and a blanket. Any sleep, any provision for aloneness that the universe may negotiate for me from the greediness of evil, was a glimpse into how little was needed for peace.

Once, old mother ocean
spoke to me —
but not in words I knew...

EIGHTEEN

GOOD MEMORIES

The Nowhere Café was one of Rafi Salcedo's good memories. His Uncle Manny had launched it as an always-open health food joint for students, brainy artsy types who liked to discuss impossible topics at night—the latest redevelopment scandal, the consequences to small businesses of raising the minimum wage, whether they would vote for the new party, and so be a national sensation at having broken the two-party system—over expresso coffee and green tea and beer; they came here because the others came, because the atmosphere was openly tolerant and they were never thrown out.

"My uncle was a dreamer. He always had a book of poetry by a Newyorican poet on the counter. Read aloud, for the right audience, bilingual poems, then a very revolutionary thing to do. On Fridays, he invited students from the college to read their own. He had success because he spoke English perfectly, not a common thing then. Was respectful of other cultures. The way he put it, if you love your culture, you will be respectful to others. It was great to come here for a snack after school. He always had banana bread and real orange juice."

"The town has changed, hasn't it?"

"I feel, almost, that I am someplace else. It is still my hometown, though. There are signs of identity; you cannot erase those. But I think that one sees more clearly the decadence of cities in these small, old ones. They built their wealth on businesses related to commerce of supplies. And with the computer age, those changed, along with the behavior of people as well. So everything closed down: restaurants, bookstores, music stores, and stationary stores. And what was left? Nobody with a vision. Emptiness revealed. Unless you have some history to support memory, the culture disappears."

"I have seen it first-hand in my street. But this is a sad topic. Look, we have things in common, for example, cool uncles." Renata was careful not to bring up her situation too often. She valued Salcedo's friendship.

"True! A toast to their beautiful spirits!"

"But he is not around."

"Oh, I see what you mean. The café has changed. Now is more like a neighborhood sandwich store. Without imagination. From eight 'til four or five. Manny sold it when he got some circulation problem that made it hard to move well. He's now in New York. Retired, writing his own poetry."

They raised their teacups and toasted.

"How did you decide to become a policeman?"

"I don't look the type, if that's what you mean. But it was a decision I don't regret. I started fooling around with psychology. I wanted to understand this or that about us, family, myself, whatever. Many clinicians start that way. I volunteered as a counselor in a church; it was part of a class project. I met a guy who was recovering from drug addiction, Ed. He wanted to talk, a validation of his experience, hoping you would not reject him as so many had done. He looked tough, motorcycle-and-beer tough, but he was gentle. He recovered memories from childhood abuse after he stopped drinking, and he wanted the world to know he was a good guy. Had a following among the motorcycle crowd. The belief he had was that he, like some among that gang of bar and pot culture, had been abused in family circles, as was confirmed by members of gangs who became his followers and that their behavior was a consequence of them having been disrespected, their space violated too early, when their personality was forming. Ed said that when he was deep into drugs, he would break into homes, businesses, or cars and destroy and take things. Just as it had been done to him."

"How interesting! There is a doctor, Gabor somebody, who claims that nobody chooses to be an addict. That one is reenacting an abuse that injured you deeply when what you needed was love and nurturing."

"Exactly. But communicating the abuse in a logical manner, even if you are good with words, is dangerous. You see what happens to you. Society is not ready to accept your version of how you started to dissociate and act differently. That Uncle Frank would come from behind, reach inside your pants, grab your thing, and whisper into your ears, 'Do you know what this is for?' And then he shows you. But you had blanked out in terror. And it happened once and again. He was bigger than you. You learned also that it was your fault and that youshouldn't tell—and what would happen to you if you did. Great Uncle Frank! The generous man who donated T-shirts and equipment to the football team. You try to fight the memories that want to come out. You cannot deal with the pain. Ed believes that drugs and drink saved him from madness until he was ready for the truth."

"What happened to Ed?"

"He was studying psychology, the last I heard. Busy with his healing, which he believed to be a life project. Like a religion. He did a lot for others like himself."

"He was absolutely right! Healing is a process; you must earn it every minute. Forever!"

"Correct. One thing he believed was that there are two kinds of people in our society: the abuser and the abused. No middle ground. He counted as an abuser the person who was a witness but was afraid of coming forward and revealing the truth. The person who prefers to lose you rather than help do justice."

"That's what inspired you to become a cop."

"Yes. I thought the police should really protect, not just punish. And to protect, you need to understand the pain from which the man who commits a crime acts. Also, not all crimes are visible. We must listen more, believe the victim."

"I don't think the chief of police agrees with you."

"He doesn't. But I hope to make a difference. Ed left such a joyful mark on me that I had to make this move. My mother thought that changing a college degree for police training was a downgrade. But my insights have helped a lot of people, for example, in domestic violence cases. Ed was describing me one day how he could not aspire to love, not until his healing opened that gift for him. Something that seems so simple as holding hands, touching the other's hair, a gentle kiss … It cannot happen because that's how the abuse started, with a leaning over and a caress. That's why I am effective in these cases because I understand the confusion and grief of the one who lashes out. The one who attacks is doing so to someone who is not in the room."

Renata was listening, weeping quietly like spring rain. "But I cannot forgive them. Whatever their pain is, it cannot be bigger than mine."

"It's not letting them off the hook. And forgiveness is a private decision. Remember what Jesus said, 'Forgive them because they don't know what they're doing.' They are so hurt themselves that they cannot do better."

Renata thought for a minute. "I have, at least sometimes, said that I forgave someone. But I didn't care about those people. It was easy to push them aside with that forgiveness that didn't change anything in my feelings for them. It was good for me to have distance. But what if there is someone you care for? How do you do it?"

Rafi looked at her in silence, with a question in his eyes, almost pleading for an answer, but didn't say anything. He had learned about privacy, limits, and respect, even if, as a friend, he had a question. Renata saw the struggle and looked down. She didn't answer. One day though, she would have to say something about Pauli the Ghost. She wanted to tell about that lovable ghost in her life, in her past.

"That is the real question, yes. The first step is you being the bigger person. It does not stop there, granted. But the realization that you are responsible for your own actions only is a powerful one. It separates you from the other in a healthy way."

Renata nodded. She needed these explanations, this guide to the intellect. She had been told so many times that she wasn't making sense, that she was imagining things, that she should be checked by a doctor, and here Rafi was instructing without attacking her. She was beginning to really like him.

Rafi was still talking about strategies he proposed, changes to laws. Renata thought all was wonderful. All would help for sure, much better than what was in place now.

"But decriminalizing in theory a criminal action does wonders for justice. Makes it easier to prosecute a case because some key people are touched and become more cooperative. They understand the objective is to improve communication; it makes people feel better about themselves. Look at your situation. Ain't going nowhere. You say what they do, and you don't know what they say to the police behind your back. But the police come back with a silence that implies that they won't help. Nasty. They don't give you a chance at justice."

"I have tried so many things! Hoping, as you say, that someone will engage his heart."

"Follow that route. You never know who will show up next."

Renata choked on her tea. She couldn't help but laugh at the idea. The case was so crazy, that thinking of one more actor was madness. But she also thought that one day somebody would be key to putting the bullies in their place by passing them a bill for their illegal actions.

"One morning in the spring, I had been working for a while on Unk's papers when I heard Hubber outside. But I had a camera there! I went out and found the sign I had placed on the wire fence—No Trespassing/No Harassing—had been destroyed and the pieces thrown over the fence. I had it on camera, which later I emailed to the police. Then I saw that the camera had been dragged down from the tree where it hanged and thrown on the ground. It had been approached from behind, so no image was shown, and I guessed it was Emmett. Those are his type of things. So, I thought all this was proof of something, right?"

"Right. At least attack on your property. Signs of ongoing harassment."

"I called, and the police sent three muscular guys. Three cars. When they saw me in jeans and with a score of music in my hand, they looked like they were wondering what was going on. Somebody in charge had the wrong idea of me."

"It must be they were worried about you and wanted to show you their feelings, with honors."

"Thank you for the humor. I brought them to the garden. They admired all the vegetation. As for the sign destroyed and the camera on the ground, the only thing one of the guys said was that they took it down because it was not on my tree."

"Was he right?"

"No. I showed where the fence was, where the tree was. It was mine. So, this guy said, 'OK, we will send you the Mobile Unit.'"

"What!?"

"Yes, I said thank you because I thought they would come to talk to me and get the story, which they didn't get. Three of them!"

"And the Mobile Unit?"

"A man and a woman, not very smart-looking. I explained what I was doing with the music and so forth. The woman, if she had been alone, I could have made her see something. But he was a bully. He kept coming close to me as if he wanted to put me inside a straitjacket. He kept asking me what I did to deal with this. I said that I call the police sometimes. I have tried to get to an agreement with the neighbors. I said that I paint and that I am writing the story. The man was beside himself. He wanted to know if I drank alcohol. I said no. I am a health freak. I do not even take aspirins."

"Yeah, looking for drugs. I guess that's their main function, using the pain of people."

"Disgusting. Sometimes I try to laugh. I tell myself that the police are just waiting for the day or night when I will kill myself. They will charge me with the crime, but since I am dead and cannot serve time, they will bury the case."

"That's funny. I mean it is horrendous. That's why it lends itself to parody."

They were silent, looking at each other after the long talk.

"I promise to think about this. I will not get involved as a policeman. But you will have your day of truth. Say, let's come here again some other day."

Renata felt a bright space opening to her. The idea of meeting with Rafi again was like a nod from her future.

NINETEEN

DOWNTOWN

Downtown, Day Off.

The furniture store he remembered, had recalled vividly with hunger as his savior, had closed. It was a huge, silent loneliness, the desolation that man's interference with space brought to our gaping eyes!

We ran expectantly, a desired armchair lovingly held in the showroom of the mind, but were confronted by the void. The other store that used to be on the little side street moved somewhere else, becoming a discount warehouse back in the woods. Where do people go to find simple, everyday objects? Everything must be locked away by now in huge containers, delivered by mail, if you know how to ask for them and where. Cities, then, are useless. We don't need anything anymore, not even one another, nor love, and certainly not conversation. There is no room for dissent, the different impacts and threatens. Our paths are divergent. There is no vanishing point organizing the perspective of the direction of our lives, where we would meet at the intersection. Time is made of scarcity.

Where did people go to meet one another? That was why Downtown crumbled, empty. We lacked safe spaces of the heart, of the mind. We had grown separated, uncomfortable with closeness.

Rafi contemplated his childhood city coldly. He had not felt this let down since he came back to fill the policeman post. In the fragmentary manner one ruminated at twelve midnight, after eight hours of brutalizing work, he did think now and then of the classmates he had not seen since that distant time when childhood and adolescence were placed as old memories in our emotions. Things had happened in other circumstances. No longer did schools bring busloads of students to have lunch at the Mexican restaurant for Culture Day; it closed down, and the building was empty. Where to find Doña Micaela, who made fresh churros from scratch there?

A simple event like that closing dispersed so many, boarding up a chapter against the intention of stability that time and history must have. At some point, we desired duration to embrace understanding, the familiar, touch, and warmth. *This moment, be still! Help me hold the divine in my hands!*

He walked up the street to the nonprofit across the parking lot, the store to benefit the homeless, where the L&G Club used to be. This was the way things were going, Rafi. In the deconstruction stage of this civilization: donating old furniture for tax breaks, selling cheap to buy dope, and buying secondhand to help out---all in the space where a legendary temple of music and innovation had been, because now there was no audience. We had emptied out our souls. What were we thinking when we started this crash? How did towns collapse? Anyone cared? What could you do, Rafi, to prop up the structure against the possible disaster, now that you had fallen in love?

Well, that was overstating something rather. What did you come here for---a new table and chairs and a decent couch? Did you get paint to transform the walls? Did you make a list for what's needed to dust, wash and keep fresh flowers?

Rafi entered the Whale Chest. The space now was called that, a place that held in its aura the embraces of dancers, the jazz piano of the Southern player that only touched the black keys.

All in your head, Rafi. Nobody remembers anything 'round here. It's a phantom town. Just concentrate on your goal. Make it a commitment. You came to find how one starts dreaming of a home.

TWENTY

EYES WIDE FOR PROTECTION

If this were madness, my own, I would welcome its happiness---for what's madness but the choice of a heart that needs release from oppression to keep beating? But there was no choice here. The creepy fog hands, the silent torturer, came searching everywhere around the house until they found my hips, sliding down to my behind, to the legs. I shook them off. Moved down the hall, to the right from where I was. I sat down. I had sensed a fear from The Monster at losing his prey, many times, at the beginning, when he wasn't sure of having all the power. Now The Monster, The Thing, was sure---and merciless---since I had reported the situation to the mayor, the police, the FBI – to nobody, really.

For the mayor, I was a nuisance because he was no good at creating solutions. The chief of police was a master at using proof against me. That's how the singing group at the shelter ended. It happened this way: The Monster had taken to coming into my darkened bathroom on the afternoons of the rehearsals, where I huddled against a corner to change my pants. Before I could put the clean ones on, he was banging the teleported energy of his senile legs against my bare ones. I was disgusted and terrified. He controlled my life exactly to the inch and the second.

The following rehearsal day, I was clever. I had rolled up a pair of pants, sneaked them into my handbag, and left in a hurry for the coffeeshop, where I entered the bathroom and changed before he could trace me. Just in time! I heard his growling as I washed my hands. Another day, I went to the library. I also fooled him, by seconds. All that I needed for victory was good planning

But I was running out of public places and decided to bring my clean pants to change at the shelter itself, in the common bathroom. I changed with the lights off, as usual for me now. When I turned the lights on and looked into the mirror to comb my hair, I heard him laughing in his ghost distance, and tapped my shoulder with his phantom energy, so that I knew he could see me.

In distress, fearing that guests to the shelter, so vulnerable, could be abused by this fiend, I started another reaching out into the State system for protection. I had to believe that the system was not so broken and that a person of knowledge and integrity could be found. I was fooling myself, but what could I do but keep trying.

That thought of The Monster at the homeless shelter gave me the idea that I must bring the issue to Human Rights. Not only was I in danger, but everybody in the shelter, since The Monster knew now how to enter. Before I placed a full complaint, I entrusted the director of the local HR branch to do something to protect the shelter against The Monster. Little did I know that instead of doing something to ensure the protection of the vulnerable guests, the director would report me to the police chief, who sent a corpulent policewoman to guard me at the rehearsal, the way prisoners are.

I was polite, even friendly to this woman. Sort of putting her in her place, although she told me she would be back in two weeks. The week in between my rehearsal was cancelled, without telling me. I showed up and the door was locked. Shelter volunteers looked out of their rooms at me and laughed. They knew something that I didn't. But I guessed, as my accessing the choir became inconvenient, and my presence at shelter celebrations was prevented. Finally, there was no funding. I could not accuse the chief of police of being indifferent. He was there for the Sotos, wherever anyone from the clan sneaked in to do harm.

The days and weeks that followed that ending of the choir I loved were marked by novel didactic rituals devised by the Sotos. I came to understand that they believed that if what I was about to witness would not teach me to stop going to the authorities, then they would have to try more of that electric shock. I had to learn my lesson. Somehow.

They started with the landline phone. It showed a local number with a name, and I answered. The Monster growled and growled while the woman, AnnaLynn, used her shrill voice in the background to support the man. Neither one said any words. Soon, The Monster hung up. I made up my mind about not answering the phone unless I read the name of a friend. Those were warnings, attempts at clarifying who the boss was. They were also signs of their fear.

I had heard that growling in one of the night ghost visits; I had retreated to the farthest corner of the house, where I crouched on pillows and blankets between a chest of drawers and the radiator, hoping The Thing wouldn't find me that night. I also had a scarf around my head, covering my nose, in case breathing was what It used as a magnet.

I fell asleep finally! All that could give signals was left upstairs: cell phone and tablet. I was alone, bundled up against Terror, safe in that faraway corner of the universe. The thump against the living room window up the hall woke me up. I don't know what I really felt, but I imagine now that I lived in a state of shock, and nothing surprised me---the way a person trapped in an underground burial ground would expect a new skeleton coming to her every night The Monster had found my whereabouts, roughly, in spite of all my planning, hiding, and cunning. That night It didn't touch me, but chose a new method to punish, traveling in slow motion down my hallway in the direction of the room where I was, but didn't enter.

With every pretended step in the virtual nightmare, It growled like a furious ogre until reaching the door. There The Thing stopped. His microphone was turned off, as if gone. I held my breath, eyes wide in the dark, for protection. It repeated the action, coming down the hall, growling, and stopping dead at the door I don't know how many times. Until dawn.

Early in the morning, I got up from the fetal position I had taken on the floor of that faraway corner lost to consciousness and stretched slowly. The hurt, frozen in my limbs, stifled a cry! Silence I must keep above all. I prepared a quick breakfast of coffee and toast, which I ate standing up in the kitchen, trying not to make noise. I caught myself looking at the still hallway out of the corner of my eye. Soon I was in the bathroom, my face over the sink, sitting on the toilet, expelling all I had eaten in a thousand years. It was as if It knew what was happening to me. That same night, finding me on the floor with cushions and blankets, all bundled up in yet another corner, put his microphone over my face, and farted until the weakening of his unspent hate made him silent.

I slept with an RF/MA-detecting device by my pillow, not because it will prove anything in my defense, but because turning on the little blinking lights when the thump against the window announces the phantom is on his way. I'm begging hope not to abandon my side.

The first night I tried this manner of self-defense, of research, whatever you name it, I called the non-emergency number at the police station, and the dispatcher said she would send somebody assigned to this area when he had the time.

I noticed the new policeman took interest in the device right away, not having seen it ever or being aware of any of the complexities that science and technology can so suddenly confront our private life with. Looking so pleasantly surprised and engaging his sense of duty, of being present in the community as essential to his job, the young policeman was grateful for having had such an interesting experience, being in training on the night shift in a quiet neighborhood. He was someone who could tell others, and perhaps Renata would get a small group of followers among their ranks and, by not rejecting her situation, come to an understanding of its origin and meaning within this new social perplexity and unrest.

The Monster had help. Junior---Speedy Gonzalez, the future elected official of my nightmare---who took my mouth's biometrics sample with a strip by quantum-jumping over my body, and also took the opportunity to bump my pubic area before being gone in a flash. He had not been much involved as of late in the heavy night raids. He showed up to help his daddy, who must tell him that, when he accessed my vagina's lips with his invisible rod after a laborious job of going down my back and my belly because I had put on two pants and a period pad and wrapped myself in plastic and a big blanket, he couldn't get there and do his prodding minute after minute and after hour, as easily as before.

The son knew that I got up, changed my getup so that the pad was always frozen, and started tapping my body to undo the job of the big bully. The son also came to wherever I went after my liberation, and taught me a lesson, hitting me hard in my lower torso with the edge of his invisible hands, the same way he used to play with my thighs.

TWENTY-ONE

BOTÁNICA

Invisible Cities

Rafi had not met Director López before the death of the Baptist minister. He saw him in person this morning at the removal of the body for the first time. This felt strange; he had known most people connected with the Caribbean Multicultural Center at some point. He must be careful now. He should not be recognized as anyone else but the policeman in charge of protocol at the scene of a (possible) crime. Any other policeman could have done the job. He was an old timer, away from *El barrio* for too long, but ready to remember, which is a form of returning. Memory and art are the real lasting dimensions of our existence. The rest is dust, forgetfulness, passing, a not-knowing. What you know is always present. And being in charge as a secret agent, to uncover this death's true story, treated by the police as homicide, will need from Rafi all he knows, literally.

The just-restored-to-underground secret agent felt happy after leaving headquarters. Meeting with Homicide, exchanging notes, and getting ready for his assignment was invigorating. But he truly didn't start living until he got deep in *El barrio*, as if he were one of those *poètes maudit* who needed the destruction of the gutter to create beauty. Heck! He grew in poverty and knew beauty, not in shiny, finished products, but in the raw spiritual strength of life called friendship, generosity, and endurance. In college, they called him the novelist. He saw stories everywhere. But he could not write fiction. He wanted the magic of experience. And you had to have both imagination and balls for that.

He turned left on the corner of Union and Colombo Street, the old campground for Italian immigrants, a bygone garden with trees grafted for the miraculous wealth of the poor, who used to grow pears, apples, and peaches from the same mother trunk. And now it was a desert. You knew people lived there because of the curtains on the windows and cars parked. But no signs of action, nobody smiling, nobody period. Did the Playpen Café exist once around here? Maybe it closed, exhausted from pretending happiness in the short rests between drunken fights.

Look! Another attempt at community: a marble fountain with running water and benches, and nobody to sit. Sometimes, a man or a woman with an amputated leg, driving one of those mechanical chairs that the alone in the world rely on, appeared, grim and unkempt, at a corner. Without looking anywhere, they lurched ahead and disappeared, even at the risk of being hit, as if wanting to have the world done and over with for good.

He had been away for too long, although the quiet house where he kept his cop costumes and his underwear, where he had slept all these mute years with his back turned to love, was quite near the Colombo fountain. By car, down the one-way street and around Colman, Rafi could be in his own bed in ten minutes. He remembered the side streets, names stored in the special places where children keep roots and signs of identity. He had been absent in the spirit more than anything.

He drove around *El barrio* in the dark. A bum rushed unsteadily to his night hideout; the drug delivery guy in his old, beat-up gray Honda was still wearing the same dark gray jacket. A cat bumped a trash can for food. Rafi was ready to start his secret sleuthing. His mind was clear, and his heart at peace. He was remembering a few lines from a book adored by a few in his college days, *Invisible Cities*. Those few used to say that he would write the next volume, *The American Invisible City*.

He devoured the poetic lines on Saturday nights at the college pub. He had memorized lines from some of the chapters: cities and the dead, cities and signs, cities and desire. He could speak those lines from the and the knowledge of what had lived before us was a good signpost them: The city must never be confused with the words that describe it. Beyond the screen of a patio, the city is shrouded in a cloud of soot and grease that sticks to the houses. In the brawling streets, the shifting trailers crush pedestrians against the walls. Falsehood is never in words; it is in things.

"I remember the poetry that reveals the intimate nature of life. I cannot write that way, but I can live the life that reveals the true nature of our social contract. And I swear to be a corrective, an artist in law, to protect the forgotten and read the book to the bullies, who always think they are wiser and will get away with murder". Rafi just said his credo, aloud. He only wished Renata were here.

Rafi headed home; this quiet time spent with memories gave the night a sweet aura, and some bitterness stored in his body like unwanted swords released its hold, making the experience a thing of knowledge. He had orders on what to do on the morrow and was ready. Turning onto Shore Street, he noticed once more that the Playpen Café, the stage of so many Friday night brawls, has closed. The space, cleaned up and divided in two, was taken over by a furniture showroom and a Botanica. He tried to remember an article about it in the paper, but it was a poetic memory, nothing with cold facts and famous names. It was pleasant, something under the heading "Urban Scene." He will find it in the files he kept on his old town. He believed in memory, and the knowledge of what had lived before us was a good signposts from where to learn. He did not feel emptiness. Rafi was selecting his guides.

Every little sign counted. Memory was a way of creating a beautiful future by contemplating our experience's pictures in our own minds, like in a gallery of art and desire, and giving them a specific and unique meaning in our lives. These neighbors at Rose Avenue didn't have memories, and that's why—maybe that's why—they did those misguided actions, as if the only possible connections now were the hurtful ones, as if gentleness and logic were outdated and stupid. The sudden, the hidden, the startled, the pleasure stolen from somebody's pain, the kick, and the punch, all that seemed to be what moved now. That's why the streets were empty, and no songs were heard.

These thoughts were the hardest thing for Rafi, that Renata could be at the mercy of those degenerates at this hour. He shuddered at the things she had already revealed, that in one day, like a cycle of hell's history in twenty-four hours, she had been assaulted by the three Sotos that he knew and that she was awakened before six in the morning by the orgasmic sounds of AnnaLynn Soto and a movement as of masturbating right over Renata's body in the attic, where she had taken refuge from her cushion den downstairs, where the Old Goat Soto searched for her most often, instantly freezing her left arm for domination's sake, and overtaking her shoulders as if with a strap, breathing hard close to her nose all the while. And in the wee hours, after midnight, covered by her plastic refuge on the old dining room rug, the brilliant future politician, Ferdinand Jr., made his appearance as she fell asleep and started toning her thighs for further pleasure with a side-of-the-hand fast massage, accompanied of the slow modern *Ohhh-Ahhh* of his signature breathing. The filthy cowards!

And nobody did anything about this. Renata had no proof, no videos and no recordings. There were no witnesses on her side, although some people knew. But more and more of them were getting into action, although not as friends. And that meant potential witnesses in an extreme judicial situation, of course.

Rafi never underestimated any possibility. That was at the root of his hope.

TWENTY-TWO

A VISIT TO THE AUTHORITIES: THIS CANNOT BE INVESTIGATED

"This is terrible!"

The mayor and his right-hand man had read Renata's complaint addressed to Betty and Emmett Sugrue, the original bullies who had been involved in daily family squabbles of their own since prehistoric days and, at some point, turned all their animosity against Renata and her uncle.

"They are so loud! And it is always the same fight!"

That's what a former neighbor from across the street would say, almost every day. He was one of those professionals at the pharmaceutical company who had become transient people with the new management. He was highly qualified but transient. And no matter how offensive, loud, mean, or drunk Betty, Emmett, and the grown daughter were, they had control of the street. They were the respectable ones.

"I just don't want them to do to me what they do to you."

That was Marsha Thomas up the street, just retired, and one of the original members of the neighborhood association a few years back—now descending now descending into becoming one of the gang, which welcomed her with open arms, especially the Sotos, next door to her, in need of validation of their new status.

Marsha, the executive secretary professional, was friends with all those less accomplished people around, dragging whatever remnants of decency were left in the street down the drain. Renata had a handwritten statement by Marsha from the last neighborhood meeting, saying that her wish was that people respect one another.

But people were not always consequent. Renata knew. Just what's expedient, easy, and comfortable. Marsha didn't want any trouble for herself. And now, Renata alone is left to understand how to live in this tangle of different stages of arrested development, failures, despair, rage, and narcissism that make up the population confronting Renata's living at her uncle's family home. Nobody had ever lived there except the family. But the gang was not to be confused by facts and called her illegal, drug user, weirdo, and invisible.

"Just get what you want and leave. You're costing us too much money," yelled Penny at her, pretending to sweep the doorstep with five furious swings of her old broom.

In response, Renata made a list of behaviors and how they violated city ordinances or laws, just what the association was for, to keep life respectful and within reasonable expectations. That's how she had redacted the paper that city officials were looking at. Any clear way of communicating what was happening was as good as another. Just start somewhere.

The concern was about the way some members of the street were treated: psychological violence, long-term harassment, safety issues, civic and law violations, ignored requests to state a concern if there is one, endless phone harassment, door slamming, name-calling, yelling, trash and dead animals on her doorstep, and the repeatedly vandalized composter and breaking of its lid.

This vandalizing was an everyday event, which implied as many instances as possible of trespassing into the garden, followed by specific dates. And since they both sat up there day and night, did they know who was doing it?

There was silence from Betty and Emmet at this important question. They knew who was doing it, and Emmet himself bragged of how many times he had been in the basement. The fear was growing in the street that one must comply with the gang and accept the mounting acts of vandalism and incivility. This made the last one to arrive very vulnerable. This silence suggested assent.

The mayor and his right-hand man, retired bank manager, Stan Fallon, looked at Renata. They had read the neighborhood association's complaint, which she wrote. Unk would have written it if he had been here. In fact, in a way, he taught her how to present a situation not easily communicable by starting with the preamble, "It has been established …" The facts, specific times, and people named—in good faith, truthfully, with the objectives of peace and understanding above all—confer the document authority. Old Marsha Thomas could support Renata, but she won't, and not for the reason she gave. Unk believed she was a spy for Betty and Emmett. She was still that spy, working from her couch, from where she made and received calls on the latest while watching TV and eating cakes.

Listed were the times when the garden camera was offline and a person tried his hand at home invasion, trespassing through the yard at number twenty-one as well, in full view of the ever-watchful Sugrue. Part of the handle was broken, like the basement door had been broken before. And Emmett boasted he had been in there many times, before fences and cameras had been installed, but this was not proof of anything, just hearsay from the victim.

"The mayor is correct; this is terrible." Mr. Fallon said one or two things that were right on the money. This was one of them.

Renata tried to guide the top officials in understanding the complaint in a creative manner, not with punitive intent. What did it say about the culture of the city that two men, neighbors, gathered under Renata's window every night as she watched a movie, and pretended to make love with the hot breathing going, while the rest of the so-called neighbors applaud and laugh? They also trespassed to do this; part of a hedge had been trampled on, cut down, in order to get cozy for their prime-time performance. They all assumed they were insulting Renata this way.

The two top men in town seemed to have a hard time thinking; they brushed aside their initial disgust and confronted Renata with tough questions: What did they say to Renata, the neighbors? What did they request from her, which she obviously didn't give them? What did she do to provoke them?

Renata insisted she didn't know what their complaint was because they had never told her. She would do anything reasonable. And she didn't provoke them. There was no communication, as this was understood in polite society. The harassing actions described are a kind of communication. But how to respond to that?

It was scary to think, how to respond. A person's life was at stake; how you reacted at that specific moment will decide so much, like in the important confrontations of myths and history, except these were just everyday life moments, banal, petty, and sordid. She went out to buy coffee at seven in the morning last Saturday. They had not let her sleep. Friday nights were important for them. When she returned with her coffee, Penny, Matt Cacelli's old woman, was waiting, sitting on a bench.

As soon as Renata stepped out of the car, Penny started mimicking a police siren while Matt kept repeating, "Leave! Leave! Leave!"

Renata wondered what the others in her street would do if they stepped out of their house and found toilet paper strewn on the lawn. Probably blame her. But they could do this action. It was part of the vocabulary of Hate Crime, but they didn't see it that way. What were they teaching the children?

Once again, Renata was saying that all this must stop immediately. Didn't you have a procedure in place for these cases? Schools had better rules. Why were councilors chosen? Will they take action?

Renata didn't let them off the hook. She said that she found it surprising that the new government, self-proclaimed progressive, was so narrow in its conception of its own possibilities to affect change toward peace. The mayor said he did not recognize the ordinances she mentioned. Renata said: "They are available on the web. But if they didn't exist, what are you waiting for!? Enact them if they don't exist! Be creative. Use your power. Look at what Lincoln himself said about situations like this one, 'As our case is new, so we must think anew, and act anew.'"

They both lowered their eyes, not considering her question, just finding ways to get out of the situation. The mayor answered finally, eyes averted, "You do it." (That meant, act. He was shaking off responsibility and telling Renata she should act.)

"This is a public safety and health issue. I don't know these people; I have never disrespected them. You have plenty of proof here that it is a clear case of biased, racist discrimination and petty criminal behavior: trespassing, kicking my fence, yelling at all times of the night, cutting my trees and dumping them on my garden, damaging locks, stealing pants from the clothesline and returning them in the morning by dumping them on the ground … How about the statement 'You are invisible'? That's textbook racist speech. You are dehumanized. You don't exist. This is a public issue, as the House of Representatives acknowledged by passing Bill One."

"I don't know anything about bills or ordinances. That's for the chief of police to decide."

The chief of police! Heart buddy of Ferdinand Soto Jr. Unk was so right! We needed professionals in charge, he said. Because the more she reported these actions, the worse things got for Renata.

The mayor was not available in the following days. Stan Fallon had made friends in city hall by telling on the sly all that the bullies said about Renata, building a smoke screen to hide how inefficient he was.

There were no state officials who wanted to receive this complaint. They had voted for Bill One because they were expected to, but they were not interested in soiling their hands to defend it against the people who voted them into office.

Renata meditated on the word Patience. She couldn't continue being patient. But what else could she do? If not for herself, she had to persevere to honor her loved ones. She had to be patient for Unk's sake, for his memory. And for Rafi Salcedo, her friend.

TWENTY-THREE
NOT IN SERVICE

"Cutting branches by hand! Nobody does that now!"

"We don't have to be like her, love. We got machines."

"She can't pay to hire workers. That's why."

"And wears brown pants! Ha-ha-ha! There she goes again!"

"Love," says the man.

And both, Ferdinand Sr. and AnnaLynn, were sort of bent, fake-crouched, by the imitation boulder they had placed as decoration on the grass near the front door. They could not kneel; weight and lack of practice prevented it. But ridiculous as they were, they found in themselves the inspiration to do a mime of yard work by hand, as Renata did for real because of her convictions. And they felt so much better about themselves for putting someone down in public, as if they had won first prize in their new neighborhood.

As soon as Unk died, the Sotos presented their bid to be leaders by responding to the call of the gang spirit settling in the street like phantom fog. They had pretended to be a good family, stating their arguments through flattery and expensive-looking cars. They showed smiles and servile bows to the people next door, overlooking the criminal actions of some because they were owners, bosses perhaps at their jobs, with some family member in the military maybe. One of them was a postman, somebody important. Of course, they'd never lived in a neighborhood like this, and it was nice- -from the apartment over the bodega in Hartford, drafty and dark, to this home with backyard, it felt they were rich. So many fools had been left behind, and a great percentage of their prayers for property been answered. No doubt this was the way.

"Hey! How you doin'! Ha-ha-ha."

Renata recognized the voices recorded on her landline phone. And he, the son, was the *Ohhhh-Ahhhh!* voice that had started to come wirelessly, pretending finding pleasure between her legs suddenly---in the wee hours, via quantum experiment way or something else, something dark and perilous. How did they get her number? This non-question by Ferdinand Jr., followed by jeering, was said against a background of mumbling older women's voices, suggesting a slandering party, the new *Aquelarre*. Only one word was allowed by the cruel gathering to be heard clearly, Renata's last name, Machado. That was the mother's voice, AnnaLynn, who obviously had gone around inquiring. The numerous anonymous crank calls were symbols left in Renata's phone, a warning by the messenger of darkness.

Impossible to return this call and answer how she was doing. The number, as would happen from now on regularly with crank calls, was not in service, or were numbers borrowed briefly from line two or similar services for anonymous callers, even barbershop numbers not in use anymore. Sensing that they would not answer her when she went across the street to their house, Renata wrote on a large piece of paper, her hands trembling with hurt,

> *If you didn't make that evil call last night, please tell me. We cannot have this behavior in the street.*
>
> > *Neighborhood Association*

She was right. No one came to the door, implicitly acknowledging they had made the call. That was the culture now. They kicked you on the sly because you deserved it. They were not to blame for anything, not that they wanted to get caught---but form their alliances on this type of social behavior, rejecting and attacking the different, the attractive. The neighbors were modeling a space where they would not be challenged, where telling on them would be impossible, where there were no questions asked and authority would be opaque and absolute. No nonsense.

There were no conversations. Their vocabulary and grammar structure would be codified by a few, and strictly followed by those who wanted to belong: remote-activated beeping of parked cars at night, fence kicking, spying under Renata's windows, slamming doors when the outcast showed at the door, shunning parties when the outcast stepped into the garden, crank phone calls, and greeting one another when the outcast was present and thus left out, punished for being.

One of the first rituals in which AnnaLynn, the mother, participated happened soon after the phone recording from her son, the student-turned-future politician. Renata would paint at night in her studio under the skylight (beyond the glass, the stars). She had been recovering old wood panels, discarded in the basement and the garden years ago. Painting them was a peaceful activity, some kind of restorative justice.

She heard a cry, yelling really, and a dog barking with anger under her window. Renata didn't want to interfere with anybody's life, and although it lasted longer than it would be natural, it stopped eventually, only that it happened again the following day exactly. The third night, Renata went down to see if she could help, just in time to see how AnnaLynn disappeared quickly behind the red truck. Matt and the dog posed in their front yard, back turned on her and curved by the burden of cowardice, as if unconcerned.

After arriving home from the library at five o'clock, a brutal voice addressed Renata from behind something, behind distance, trees, shadows, and the darkness of ignorance.

"Come up here!" It was an ugly roar, guttural, the expression of primitive beings. It was repeated three times, and then silence. There was no narrative supporting their distress, their ignorance, or their anguish at having to contemplate the active, kind Renata.

"Tell me. What happened to you? Why this recurring wound?" She says this aloud, to nobody. But Renata felt that if she would be listened to, she would go up and ask the question of the man who just yelled at her in a manner that didn't expect anyone responding.

February 11, 6:02 a.m.

Renata wrote the following note, because she had to do something. She needed a witness, if only a piece of paper. Would it be a good idea to give it to Rafi Salcedo?

"I just came up from making coffee. I have been typing Unk's memoirs since four thirty this morning. I slept on the rocking chair quite well for about four hours! Now, Old Goat's action has started, mimicking orgasm movements under my butt. I put cushions all around to protect myself."

TWENTY-FOUR

A PINKERTON MAN AND THE PARANORMAL GUYS WHO COULDN'T BE WITNESSES

Renata wasn't exactly sure who proposed a private investigator, but it was through an acquaintance at the voter's registration office, maybe even the mayor's right-hand man, that Mr. Dupuis, Dup for friends and customers, came into this mess. She was so desperate that even parting with money was welcome, if someone said he had the tools for action and revelation, anything but this accumulation of aggressions, this endless being at the mercy of the charity counselor and his gang, the Bettys and Emmetts of the world. Anything, but being chained to this absurd suffering.

As in fairy tales, danger was not a thing of one day sometimes, or of nighttime, but an oppression that enslaved, the story your path was made of. The Monster-counselor got his hands on your butt or breast or got into bed with you with his virtual body, piercing your genitals with an invisible pointed object. Nightmares didn't take time off. They were like hunger in the slums.

Their first meeting was so friendly, at city hall. A smile and some well-thought-out strategies were all Mr. Dup needed to earn his first five hundred. Easy. He told Renata of the time when he asked his boss in the police not to wait too long to start looking for the missing teens, and thanks to his urging, they found them and their car at the bottom of the river, dead but found. Otherwise, they would have been missing for a long time, forever.

That was good. It showed, on paper at least, that he cared. Every minute was significant. You were important to him. Even more, he had dug up from memory's slippery archives that story about the American diplomats being spied on the sly—more than that, secretly from some kind of advanced invisibility science trick—by foreign agents while on peace negotiations in Havana. Or probably it was Nicaragua. They were in the same room, but invisible. Although they could be felt, that's how the diplomats knew there was something not right, the invisible presence, as Shelley put it. Somebody important had had the experience of being faced with invisible beings. Then Renata was not the only person in the world with this experience, apart from the actress in *Invisible Man*.

"It was not so crazy after all," Dup said in an afterthought.

And so he got his five hundred and said that now the situation was in his hands. The investigator will do his thing. Silence, please. And with that, Renata left for her rehearsal, lighthearted, happy, and inventive. If she had bought herself a toaster, which she needed, she would probably have felt guilty at the expense. But Dup would deliver her from The Monster and his family, with the help of those five hundred.

The courthouse date approached, and the monsters—Old Goat, the promising politician Jr., and now, AnnaLynn herself—were especially active. Dup had been at the house once, posing as a man who installed propane heating units. He arrived on Sunday afternoon with a backpack and a new children's hard hat, green, as if ready for prime time for the whole family. Everyone was there, bored, after church and lunch, not that it was planned that way. It was an unclever show that gave Renata much pleasure while it was happening and plenty of grief afterwards. Dup never knew about the aftermath because his job was to show up that one time. Done!

Renata had explained that the intrusion was wireless, no gadgets or wires. Nothing. It was like all coming from the cloud and the universe, quantum physics.

Ah, yes! Like the toaster! He had looked that much up. But when he came to the house, he spent a lot of time passing his rod over everything, including the chimney, like looking for hidden treasure. Renata let him do it. Probably he was thinking. But he wasn't. No signals of wires or devices, he informed, which was known in advance.

He looked at all the rooms. He asked for the function of the old bedroom, now a place to store clothes and to spend time on the rug reading and watching movies. He looked with interest at the closet and old drawer. He looked around the garden with admiration and wondered out loud where the propane stuff would go, just to give the neighbors something to think about. Hubber at least was thinking right, and when Renata was in the attic later, he threw one of his invisible projectiles against the wall by the futon, although she tried to reason with him. She asked him whether anything about the visit to the attic had upset him. Were they too loud?

Renata even gave Dup the garden key because he said he would look at something special there, like talking to the neighbors and seeing if anyone would say something.

No. But he didn't specify what he wanted to look at. Renata explained again: the harassment comes from specific neighbors who come in wirelessly, not in person.

The next time she called, Dup was not available. He even hung up on her when she was leaving a message. By the next time they talked, a lot of things had happened to Renata, and Dup did not know any of them. What happened was not his focus, just the passing of time and his budget. He texted to say that the guys with the special listening machines, the paranormal guys, advanced, with x-ray-type photo capability, were ready to come Sunday night after dark. Although none of them worked Sundays, they were doing this for Renata.

"Are you having paranormal experiences?"

Renata had found the two guys in the street earlier than it was expected, waiting for Dup. She asked them to lower their voices because as soon as they said that magical word, there was a lot of expectation in the air. They came into the house without Dup.

"There is a ghost in the hall!"

The younger of the two guys came running into the kitchen, not believing himself, touching his body and very pale. But Renata knew The Monster-Old Goat-Soto had been there. She saw him. She and the other guy laughed for different reasons. Renata knew it was true but could not say it without giving them more reasons to believe she was crazy. At that point, they seemed to her like nice people, before she looked into her top drawer, for example.

They were with their electronic briefcases in the old bedroom, where the Old Goat ghost mainly showed up, living there day and night, wanting to catch Renata undressing. Their rod hummed continuously, and a flash went off at times and took photos. They wanted to do the work without other presences because the living could bring in their energies and spoil the results.

"We should leave them alone to do their work because our energies could mix with the ghosts, and the quality of the work was likely compromised."

Dup signaled Renata to join him at the living room table. He thought the guys left by themselves in the old bedroom were great and insisted they had encountered ghost signs and much more. Such energy and meaning! While this was happening, Dup took the time to tell Renata that he spent two frigid nights down by the apartments, bundled up, with his camera, just in case someone tried to enter the house. (They became three frigid nights later, and it was a mild winter.) The existing camera was facing the door in plain sight.

These were the nights Renata took refuge at the social service agency, stayed at the hospital until one in the morning, and so forth. A part of the back fence was broken around that time. The car was burglarized two days later. There was a camera by the front door. Why spend time doing this? Dup didn't answer these objections, nor the question of what to do with the wireless invasion because she was desperate and receiving no help.

Did he call Hubber Dixon to see whether he could reveal what science application the Sotos were using to assault her? Other women were down the street, young people who could become the next victims. This issue was a public health one. Could Dup look into the possibility of establishing the long-term harassment case by talking to the people that his friend knew?

"No. I didn't want to show my cards."

What cards? Renata thought to herself. But she decided against showing impatience or mistrust. Her case was too desperate to show negativity against anyone. Still, she tried to get Dup to do something, to do the job he had promised.

"But they all already guess we are doing something. Young Soto was furious the first time you came. He was tracking me on my walk after you left."

Dup did not believe Soto Jr. had the means to track Renata, but he didn't say this with words, hoping that Renata would pay anyway. They all said good night in a good mood. The ghost-picture guys seemed to like Renata, but the story itself made them uncomfortable. Or something made them uncomfortable. (Renata would have some ideas of her own later, when the paranormal guys vanished into thin air, taking with them important answers and whatnot. But with whom could she share any thought, any hurt?)

Dup texted later and said the guys captured lots of energy out of one of the rooms, the front room, where they had not been. They would take a lot of photos and stuff. As it turned out, there were no photos, and weeks later, Dup asked her to come to the parking lot of a hotel in the middle of town to receive the paranormal guys' study, for privacy's sake. There was no report, just something for fools in "Dup stationary," just his name several times, his company, fax number, and a few repeated lines about having done the examination of the rooms and encountering two ghosts who live there and a woman asking for help.

"There is no woman in my house but me. And I am asking for help. Nothing new."

"They can come back and do a more exhaustive examination. You can call them."

Renata said she thought their work was very interesting, and that was it. Dup was a bit disappointed. He thought he had made it with the ghost hunters or something.

There was a story there. Probably Dup had not paid them enough, or there was some conflict involving who would get what. With Dup, there was nothing clear. He seemed to think he had done his job. Renata did not want to get him off the hook.

No, the paranormal guys cannot be witnesses. One of them had seen the ghost. But coming forward and revealing what they saw could put them in a strange place: the place of truth, justice, revelation, and responsibility.

Dup couldn't do this job, and the paranormal guys would have to grow in spirit. What happened to Renata was not their business. They had showed up, that was their job.

But the ghosts didn't abandon Renata that night. They had their own plan, and as soon as the investigators left, they showed up by the piano, as ghosts, the whole bunch. Only that Renata recognized them somehow. She was not surprised, as if she had thought all along that would be the normal thing for the neighbors to do.

"You, Old Goat of a fake counselor! Get out of my house!"

And It left, maybe ashamed at being rejected in front of the others. But there was another one in front of Renata just as suddenly as The Monster vanished.

"I don't know you."

It was true, probably it wasn't. The woman who was at Hubber's these days, sort of masculine and a bit stocky without being fat. Whoever it was, that one left also. Hubber maybe saved his appearance for later, for when Renata was asleep, which is when he came many nights in his elegant black costume, Superman-style without the macho overtones.

But the promising future politician was there, jumping around with his pyrotechnic outfit, flashing lights, and even a candle.

"You sit there! Help me do my homework---public affairs jerk!"

And when Soto Jr. heard Renata giving these orders and pointing at her rocking chair, he broke out of his pretended self-assurance and ran away. He had been recognized! To all, she said, "Come on, guys! Can't you see I'm working?"

She had her laptop on, playing the Bee Gees at full volume, and continued writing her story. Occasionally, she could sense over her shoulders a presence, one of the ghosts trying to make sense of what she was putting down, afraid maybe that she would tell.

Notes on progress.

The paranormal guys came in February, and it's March 28. Old Goat just tried to rape me from behind, from his other dimension ghost reality. He had bothered me the whole night, and by eleven in the morning, I could not do more work. So, I stretched out on the futon, covered by two blankets. The plastic was downstairs. I fell asleep. About twenty minutes later, I awoke with disgusting fat legs touching mine, whatever reproduction of the real trash that a quantum ghost can bring to the second dimension, close to me from behind, pretending an orgasmic trembling, and the pointed wire pushing to get in my anus through the pants cloth. I got up instantly, and he had been following me since then around the house, angrily confronting me with his stinking breath.

Everybody knows this is going on---that something like this has been happening for a while. And nobody helps, having been convinced that they have no authority, that there is nothing they can do under the present laws, that they could get in trouble, that life is organized differently and things like the ones I'm describing are not possible, that they are not the people I should be contacting for help, that the authorities know how to deal with all problems.

Really, can't I just forget about this crap? What am I talking about?

Booked

"this is my town, my city. closed off and asleep. separated from me.

I cannot reach it from where I am, This city where I have been happy."

Robin Frink 4/17/23

TWENTY-FIVE

BOOKED

January 17, Midnight.

I could always think of blaming the Sotos for having a plan to push me with their daily bodiless home invasion to do something that could bring me trouble. But even if they could wish for something that required some mental discipline, I can't blame anybody. The decision was mine.

I was taking action to stop the Old Goat's endless nonsense, and so restore peace in my home. But how to take appropriate action in the world of the invisible and the crafty?

It was past ten on January 17, maybe eleven already. I had organized my sleeping place that night on the pretty rug of the old bedroom, with pillows and many blankets, plus the big plastic sheet covering it all, sure protection against the nightly sexual assault incursions of the old counselor. I was opening a book, quite pleased to be alone for once. Then my thigh was pinched, and the pointed fog hand went straight for my pubic area.

I rebelled instantly but didn't just push him out or anything. I knew what to do. I had on a shelf nearby the oversized male underwear, which most likely were too small for the brute, next to the huge bra for AnnaLynn. I had bought them late in December the day I reported the Sotos to the police for being in my bedroom with their parabolic microphone or whatever gadget they use to trespass without being seen. They are heard, though. Everything.

The oversized intimate clothes, buying them with a plan to confront, made me feel free and creative, with a future in my struggle to prove the unprovable with the tools I had. I went out of the store with the shopping bag containing the dynamite, talking to myself, imagining I was throwing the stuff at them in the middle of the street, in front of their house, as they prepared to go to church on Sunday:

"Eh, Mr. and Mrs. Counselor, you left these in my bedroom last night."

The joys and dangers of a theater education! But from my point of view, this was an attempt at clarification, at justice. They didn't acknowledge to the police that they were doing it. But even that night, after they reported me and I was taken for fingerprinting to the station, when I came back after two in the morning, the old fool didn't wait a second and came right away to jump into bed with me, hooting in triumph. As if I should be happy that he wanted to be with me---, a criminal now thanks to him, who was inviting me, touching my breast, to giggle with pleasure with him. It was hard to imagine what this imbecile thought, behaving like an obsessed degenerate but presenting himself as the respectable party.

The policemen were friendly. I didn't know why I had been arrested. I told them that this situation should be investigated because the man and the son (and soon enough, the wife, AnnaLynn, as well) kept on with the sexual events every night in the wee hours and at dawn. Do you know what that means in the life of a person, in your own home?

"But what you say is crazy. That cannot happen."

Getting ready for the walk from the house to the waiting police car was complicated. First, the Latino policeman told me I could not go alone to get dressed because I was arrested. I invited him in while I put on my brown sweater. Then it was the question of what to take with me, my keys and identification. But the question again was whether I could carry my recycled pouch full of junk—receipts, six dollars, debit card, and some change—because it could be dangerous, and one of the policemen took charge of it.

Then the Latino policeman told me I had to pay one thousand dollars, and I said, "Fine. Let me take a check." But the other cop explained I would be asked to appear in court and, if I didn't show up, I would have to pay.

That fantasy of talking to Mr. and Mrs. Counselor wasn't carried out. Instead, I took the underwear and a super-duty magic marker that tragically I had bought at Home Depot, not knowing why. But I bet my distressed intestines were already plotting some revenge. I wrote in block letters: COUNSELOR SOTO IS NOT WELCOME IN LADY'S ROOM. OUT!!

And I placed the thing on the first step of the stone staircase to that spiritually sordid home. I did not trespass; all was done from the street. And all was true. I was pleased with myself. For now, the ghoul was gone, although in a short while the poem I was reading fell from my consciousness like a wall collapsing in an earthquake. Loud, inappropriate banging was being done to my windows, to my door. Why not ring the bell? I got up, wearing my glasses and holding the poems. The policemen, all young, were laughing. The Latino one asked me in Spanish, "*¡Dónde conseguiste eso!? Lo compré para la ocasión.*"

"I bought it for the occasion," although I never thought the occasion would be this one.

I invited them to come in. They liked the pictures on the wall. They asked what was going on.

"The same. I report the old fool or the son, and they don't stop. I am trying to communicate this to them. This cannot go on forever. I have done everything that can be done to stop it, including going to their door, which they don't open. I even answer the phone when they do hang-up calls, in the hope it is a real call for conversation. Nobody should be subjected to this behavior as a life program. Something should be possible to do through the law."

"The trouble is you cannot prove it."

"But the police should have a way of finding out."

I was alone in the big car behind a wire partition. This was my town, my city, closed off and asleep, not indifferent, separated from me. I couldn't reach it from where I was, this city where I had been happy. I could be far away and remembering it, stretching out a hand but unable to touch it.

When the car stopped in the basement and the policeman opened my door, I sensed he was ashamed. He guided me upstairs where a young officer and a Latina recruit in training were waiting for me. I was talkative. He took down information on what the pouch had, and the woman recruit searched my body, the old yoga pants pockets.

The officer asked me whether I was a personality in town. Thinking of Unk, his teaching, and his music and the manuscript I was organizing, I said yes. I was a personality and the only surviving member of a civic idea, a neighborhood association, a creation for which members shared what they had left of hope and integrity. Whatever happened after those meetings died away, and it was a concern, because I was arrested for defending the idea, alone, in a hostile world.

I was caught in the friendly atmosphere in which the young Latino woman was learning the right way to get a valid fingerprint, practicing with my hand many times. I joked that I felt I was the most famous criminal in the city, with so many pictures being taken of me. Reminded them that maybe all this fingerprinting is obsolete now, since more and more crimes are being committed wirelessly on the internet.

The older officer nodded and then said, "Everything helps." Taking my photo, he asked about the color of my eyes. He liked them. Considerate, he returned my glasses quickly.

And I felt envious of this woman and anybody else who was brought by design or chance into his care. Why not me? Why wasn't this policeman assigned to my case?

As the officer finished the paperwork, he told me about the court date and the fine I would pay if I didn't show up.

"I will certainly show up. In a way, I am glad we are having this meeting with a judge or prosecutor. I have asked for something like that many times."

"Have you reported anything before?"

"Many times. And I am surprised I was brought here tonight. I thought I was asking for a conclusion of the harassment, something that should have stopped when I reported them formally. It looks like there is no record of all my complaints."

The officer looked at me. He seemed to be thinking the same as I was, why my complaints had not been recorded as completely as they should have.

They called a taxi, and I arrived home after two in the morning. In a few days, my name would be in the newspaper, in the police logs.

I laid down on the cushions where I was reading poetry yesterday, a few hours ago, an infinity ago. And It, the Old Goat, the Monster, the Abuser, tried to join me right away. He had just reported me to the police for my asking him to stop this. I was arrested, and he didn't waste time in continuing what I was blaming him for. I cursed him and went to the attic bed, me, a criminal for having unmasked him.

I invoked the magician to my consciousness. *Language, open your mysteries to me! Give me the balm that cures all injuries of the spirit, that nourishes the body to become whole again, despite the wounds inflicted by The Monster.*

How disturbing the thoughts that stumbled through my mental space! He, the overweight counselor, saw me taking off my bra and changing into my yoga clothes. He knew in which room I was, where I stored my things, what I was wearing. I sat at my desk, and he came from hidden quantum space, grabbed my thigh, and blew dirty clouds on my face. All the air around the counselor stank. I brushed my teeth in a dark bathroom for fear Ferdinand Sr. was ogling again. I calculated when he might be asleep to take a rushed shower by myself, just by myself in the middle of the night, in darkness.

I moved back and forth on top of the cushion to disturb the wireless invader. I called him filthy, stupid, idiot, and castrated. Why didn't he leave me when I despised him?

But the more I pushed him out, the closer he snuggled near me. He made little noises, too. He snored, smacking his lips like a child who just had sweet milk. I didn't wish to analyze the brute, just destroy him. Every day, I got my hideout ready on the old rug by the garden window, blankets, coverlets, and the long piece of durable plastic, well organized, to prevent the brute from getting inside and touching my behind. I went to the kitchen to pour tea, and the force was touching my back, so close that if it pushed a little stronger, I could fall. Hideous! Destroying moments of peace, that was on what evil lived, on chaos and disorder.

Soon after, I settled down, to meditate with peaceful music and take notes for tomorrow. I heard the thump on the window and knew for sure that tonight I would tell the bastard something extra, although he was not afraid. His Ferdinand Jr. will protect him from the harm of justice and law. What was the law to him? Move over, nobodies of the world!

He announced himself by blowing over my face the fetid breath, and started to place himself, or his solidified shadow, or an invisible 3D copy of his future sarcophagus, over my left leg, actions that came too close one after the other to react quickly. I repelled him with foul language, but he didn't care. He was enjoying himself, safe from the law.

———

Getting ready for the choir rehearsal, I put a bottle of water in my backpack, and the phone rang again. Anonymous once more, always when I am getting ready to leave, when entering the bathroom, when going far from the landline phone. I knew who was calling, didn't answer. But later, I checked, and yes, there was no number there. Couldn't call back either.

While walking in the corridor to the bathroom, invisible arms reached down from the air and grabbed my breasts. He laughed. The Old Goat was able to invoke laugher to celebrate harming someone.

I didn't take a shower for fear the Old Goat could see me in the dark. I took my pajamas off one piece at a time and washed at the sink, covering myself with my house coat. It was two in the afternoon, and at the homeless shelter I would be safer.

It was when returning home for the night that the danger started, without time out for peace.

TWENTY-SIX

DIARY. TERRORISTS. IDENTITY PRINTS.

While getting ready for court, there is nothing the Old Goat's ghost lenses do not spy on. Or probably it's the son, since the feeling I have of the invisible movement around me is different and more accomplished: a camera moving steadily and stopping at my shoulders, choosing specific focuses, getting in front of my face, clicking fast, without noise but perceptibly by my ear when there is something the observer does not like, such as my researching one of the harassing phone numbers. There is a gasp, or a hissing sound, on the other side of this hell. They do not approve of my awareness; it would be easier for them to trick me if they could burn my brain the way they have tried often. They track everything: what I'm writing, the movements of my mouth talking to myself, and when I'm on the phone. They act nervous, afraid, and worried. These emotions move the Sotos. Although I am the defendant who in a few hours is to appear as the guilty party in front of the judge of the world, they know I'm not the criminal in this shadow scuffle. The truth bothers them, and everyone who walks in integrity is an enemy.

Anything new about their kind of terror? Is there anything different in its texture, in the sad afternoon of its presence? It's always the same in essence. The Old Goat hounds me in the house day and night, blows on my nose so I know it's him, grabs or pierces my pubic area if I don't have my plastic shield around my body, he dishonors my breast if I'm not on guard, bumps my behind when cleaning the bathtub, hounds my head when doing the dishes, and blows on my mouth when I eat my oats alone in the old kitchen. He fashions a clumsy metal headpiece in the world of the remote power of the indecent, hooks it up to some grid, and turns it on, hoping it would burn my soul.

There is nothing new in the everyday of terror. And I'm sorry if this sounds blind to those whose bodies are maimed, crushed, incarcerated, abandoned to hunger, and bleeding.

They believe—it must be that, by the way he does things, they all go on this belief—that they are protected by respectability, by the son's connections. He grows swollen and mean with every one of their acts unexamined, just as the list of their misdeeds grows and the dull thickness in their misunderstanding of the disgust their reign inspires gives them an unexplainable pleasure, a slimy sense of power.

Terror is the absence of consolation. Pauli the Ghost is now gone, maybe because I mentioned love, such a scary prospect to his creator. Love and Pauli are exiled together. I am alone with terror, but with beauty as memory, that giver of strength, the unshakable path, my secret. There's the insistence on attacking as life's program. That's it. Attack. Throw the other on the clutches of fear. That's your only power, Monster!

He's by my shoulder, tickling the side of my face if I write something I shouldn't, according to the tyrant. So I free myself through language. I improvise a discurse on pedagogy: *Para una persona sin un tipo de educación cuidadosamente estructurada para desarrollar las necesidades de crecimiento del individuo entero—no solo del aspecto académico de asignaturas que se consideran esenciales o importantes, sino de todas: la educación física ha de tener su filosofía, como la clase de composición ha de tener su ritmo y su voz.*

This experience is both marvelous and terrible, escaping the vigilance of Big Brother by improvising content in another language on an unrelated theme, to escape vigilance and the inquisition. Language and the mind are the real roads to freedom.

Maravillosa, porque el lenguaje me ha mostrado una vez más el camino de la libertad, de las posibilidades de la vida. Terrible, porque el monstruo me espía y se apodera, en vano por supuesto, temporalmente, de manera ilegal e indecente, de mi espacio privado. Le roba la alegría a mis ángeles, que lloran, pero se hacen amigos, encuentran conmigo una lucha consistente en favor de la decencia. Esto es Terror. Es terrorismo.

First, I find the definition of *terrorist*. Soto is a terrorist.

Terrorismo: dominación por el terror. Sucesión de actos de violencia. Imposición. Invasión de morada. Apoderarse del cuerpo.

A terrorist then is the counselor for the poor.

What a great space this is, my writing, where I can take refuge and escape from oppression. It does not matter that what I'm writing now is something I had not planned, but it is dearer than anything else I labor and treasure because these lines are born out of the need to flee from the terrorist tyrant, the one who defiles your sacred private space, reaching with his hands of fog for your mouth, your legs, and your breasts. He spies on what you're saying aloud or just wording in silence a prayer, asking the angels to release you from this. He looks at what you write, tracking you to see where you go, but he cannot get into the shrine of your imagination. He cannot destroy that happiness.

You still have the strength to get up in the middle of the night and shake your body, tapping it to break down the invasion's structure. You dream of freedom and write down that dream to hold on to, like a promise of hope. You become a mirror of all the other times in history when the free spirits sang to defy their monsters, and think of Victor Jara, singing as his body was being maimed, cut up, invaded.

After this, what else can I say about terror? Could a long list of their misdeeds and the days and their time make a deeper impression? What worse terror than having the terrorist glued to your body, eternally? And nobody does anything about it. How could decent people act? By working with you to reveal the reality of what is happening. That's a thing they fear, the unmasking of the disturbing. We are supposed to live in the time of reason, of order, of laws.

Two black cars and a U-Haul unit were parked in Soto's driveway shortly after that first court appearance. I was drawing the curtains when Soto Jr. came out to greet one of the newcomers, dressed in black all of them. They shook hands, and all went in. About three in the morning, I woke up. My feet felt almost paralyzed, but that was not all. Electrical signals were going up my legs from the soles, as if from wires evenly placed in a mold somewhere else. I heard distant beep-beep, slow and rhythmic, such as those from a medical recording machine that analyzes patterns. I went outside, and from inside the U-Haul, the beeping stopped.

That's how Old Goat finds me sometimes, by checking my feet with his bodiless wire. I push him away if I'm awake. When I'm walking, they can use the tapping on the head and even the breathing of my thorax.

I now have many signs of identity. What will it be tonight? What will it be? The continuous listening to my body, so the slight movement is broadcasted to the neighborhood by their group connections.

There's the burning of my skull and the squeezing of the lungs, so badly that I feel I am about to stop breathing. What new torture? What terror still unknown to me would be capable of finally delivering my inert body to the Sotos, and record it in triumph for their eternal gloating on the dark annals of the gang?

TWENTY-SEVEN

WE ARE TRAINED ON PRETENDING

We go one by one,
out the door to the porch
down the steps to the street,
one by one …
We pass, looking down,
looking back, looking up
looking by …
We're trained on pretending.
we're just not afraid …
Never all for one,
One for all.[2]

Where did I hear that song? If music is from one place specific, so that when a person hears it he can say, 'I'm from there!' This song is from here and speaks to me. I must find it …

The idea, the awareness really, that a home could be a different thing to each person came to Rafi Salcedo recently, very suddenly, during one of his police visits. He didn't dwell on it for long. It wasn't pleasant. One got through the day the best way one could, with the understanding that the answers we gave said a lot about us.

I have been in nursing homes before, he thought. At least he had driven past them. This time, he was called to document a fight between two residents, men in their late forties. They lived in a nursing residence the way one lives in a rooming house, with less privacy but with imposed control. They were in rooms with double occupancy, whose doors were usually open during the day to the busy hallway. They complied with the schedule. They liked to be told when the attendants would come to sweep the floor and when they could have breakfast and lunch. And they had a choice of eggs

---

[2] Lyrics from "Tenants," a song by Charles Frink

or pancakes. There was order, a TV set, prescription drugs for anxiety, bodies around, and no one to yell at them.

That's all that a child needed, a safe home. That's why these residents, these inmates of the spirit, came here to live, as if it were in a voluntary manner, to die while they were still young because they could not grow into the danger of adult life out there without a home. They had the same complaints always, the same fears with the same words, and the same phrases to complain someone was talking shit about his mother again, that he was watching on TV a show he didn't like, and he was paying for that TV as well, and the police should know that he, the other, made that noise again in the morning, for which he should be ashamed.

"Officer, how many times have I told him so?"

"You gonna be kicked out! Tell him that, Officer."

"But we are friends. Honest."

"Yeah, hear him! Hear him! He's honest. Don't believe him."

"I'm not? Do you want me to leave? You won't have anyone to fight with then."

"Yeah. I guess that's right. I should consider that point."

"Thank you, Officer. We'll resolve this for real. This time is the last we argue."

The command "evolve!" should be mandatory around here, thought Salcedo, who didn't contribute a thing to the dialogue. *Or probably not. It should be prohibited, gagged by sleeping pills and television. Let them be children forever if that's their mission.*

Returning to headquarters, he dialogued with himself. The pair of friends who aged together in the nursing home was touching. Their difficulties raised serious questions.

"I'm like them. But they've come clean and said it. While I'm pretending to be mature, have a job, and be well-adjusted; I look around the place where I live, and I'm ashamed. I want to bring someone into my life, but I have no home to share, just a dusty hole with a hard couch coming apart."

"Would I be like those two at the residence, complaining about the other's presence as if it were an insult, never attuned to her rhythms, that special poetry of space and meaning that each one of us is, the thing that we fall in love with, that miss, that long to hug?"

"It is good that you are thinking all this, Rafi, disturbing as it is."

"For awareness' sake. So that if something happens, you can fall back on this reflection and don't make the mistake, the one you fear so."

"Or to be more paranoid."

"Aren't I too old for love?"

"Isn't love itself an outdated concept?"

"Get your thoughts in order, Rafi. You are at work. Make everything SMART: specific, measurable, achievable, relevant, timely. Like school goals."

"And that's what they convince us that reality is. So, when we reveal our profound dissatisfaction, loneliness, yearnings, and discontent, we have mental health issues, not philosophical concerns or social and spiritual needs. That's vague. Calling somebody crazy is so much more specific and timelier!"

"Stop right there, Rafi. You are arriving at headquarters!"

TWENTY-EIGHT

THINGS ARE GETTING SERIOUS:
THE STATE COURTHOUSE

What are we all doing here? I've passed this building so often. I came frequently next door with Unk to the little theater, and he played the piano there. Someone said once this was the state courthouse, but I thought nothing of it. "Nice building," I said, inspired by castles with Gothic turrets and low windows in the back, suggesting unimaginable harsh prohibitions and hidden punishments.

And now I am here, inside, a reported criminal, waiting my turn to answer the judge in the auditorium-like courtroom, next to drug dealers, illegal gun owners, and users, next to inmates out of their cells to stand once more in front of the judge to hear again the verdict that they are no good, and wait handcuffed and guarded for their return to jail, next to thieves and abusers out on probation wearing their head low, standing by their expensive lawyers.

I admire the body of a man in handcuffs standing with his back to an almost-full house of people in trouble plus the cheerful public who have come voluntarily looking for a cheap laugh at the expense of the guilty, a beautiful man maybe younger than he looks, submissive for the moment, saying a musical "Yes, Your Honor, I understand" to the stiff and dissonant voice of the judge who growls that if he sells pot once more, he will lose his rights. Why are we here blaming one another, locking each other up, instead of working to make our lives together bearable?

So many people milling about, the prosecutors in and out of doors with folders, busy without time for anyone who might need their attention. They are worried—with pasty, chubby faces and bodies that one imagines uncomfortable with any other life but this one of corridors, guards, courtrooms, file cabinets, and people charged with shady crimes who turn to lawyers and public defenders to justify them or to claim not guilty with a heavy heart and lack of conviction. But I … what am I here for?

The prosecutor opens the folder and doesn't see any accusation. She cannot guess either why I am called to this dark vault of guilts and punishments. She mumbles something about concerns about my mental health, trying to make sense of sheet after sheet I haven't seen nor who is the author of the lines confessing so much false concern for me.

Why not? I think. *If that's the only recourse they have to hide their crimes from the law …*

My mental health and the phony bill from Soto's friend garage are unexplained and unusable as a crime, and so this is a felony that Soto, the chief of police's friend, committed. Creating a fake invoice would give him five years, and a few more for sneaking it into the courtroom as if it were real.

"Don't you have a lawyer to walk you through all this?" says the prosecutor.

"What is this?" I ask.

I have been called twice already to face the judge, and I am not told what I am accused of. The prosecutor sends me upstairs to get a public defender, but I don't qualify. This is for the poor: a long list of the names of young people typed next to their charity lawyer propped on a counter for anybody to see.

What a way to start the day! I think, looking at two good-looking young men, barely old enough to be counted as men, wearing their tight, unwashed jeans and staring at nobody with big eyes and a questioning smile, like saying, "What!" Trouble and loss are written all over their tender-and-getting-chunky bodies, needing already some weed. I think Soto is dangerous, but really, I have no idea what danger is.

Young punks and Latinos have stalked me. My car has been slightly damaged twice, once after each time I didn't pay the eight hundred. Plus, the wooden fence in the back was broken, each one on time to show rage for my release from the courthouse. They let you go; you'll see now, threatening in the shadows, fanning the flames of fear, nothing spoken and clarified. The son walking in the dark under my fences, following my light or my body signals, mumbling something late at night after his party meeting, as if I would respond to the dictate of tyranny just because he's so important.

This is my study in terror, crime, and danger; disturbing, but those categories or characteristics are not inside me. Nothing can tempt me to take them seriously or give them in my life more thought or time than a concern for safety requires.

Something about my attitude wins for me freedom in the courtroom. Anyone so sure of her innocence, but ready for a verdict even if she has not been accused of a crime, must be allowed to go free. But the real criminals are not here.

They are free but alone, without the consolation of getting a chance at illuminating the souls of the condemned, of being the harbinger of freedom to the community and all the rituals of joy we have forgotten for how to celebrate with our neighbors.

They are free but alone, with the Sotos and their hangers-on, who always have followers, summoning one another to the bully page online to learn what happened to me: Did I pay? When will I be jailed or thrown out of town? While they still have not resolved anything: they stir up discord against me among anyone who will listen, and which the prosecutor has specially prohibited; they have crafted a false invoice, a felony, and used the wonderful court system to try to cash it from gullible me, using the system to steal. They are the real criminals.

I doze. In the Reign of Danger, pretending there is any time at all when the conditions are other than dark and perilous is irresponsible. Although I have a blanket rolled between my legs, cushions on top of my behind, and huge plastic over all my body, including my head, Soto Jr., the future great politician, jumps from the window, enveloped in a flash of his ghost persona's great-time-signature white light and magic wand with pyrotechnic halo for the occasion. He goes right for my private parts, advised where I was by his father. He tugs at my security belt of a rolled blanket and yells. I hear the voice, complaining, thin, removed, and sense the invisible hands pulling at the blanket, but I don't allow him and get up: something I'm learning. It is four thirty in the morning, and darkness stares, serious, as if blaming me for the disgusting scene, as if staying tense and awake could have prevented his violence, intrusion, and anger.

TWENTY-NINE

LIBRARY FOR RANDOM WISDOM

He filed the ball court complaint once more. The lady argued the players were violating city noise ordinances by playing ball after nine in the evening. They claimed they made no noise. The police were wasting taxpayers' money on pretended time, when the real problem was intolerance and bigotry, all getting much worse the more cops you threw into the fire. Get a priest! A conflict resolution worker! The police didn't want to hear that. It had been proposed in several interesting ways because, the boss argued, there is no danger and that no one will die. And they dreamt of this conflict and more conflicts to come, to ask for more cops, more money, and more Tasers. Restorative justice would not flourish in this concrete garden.

In this wasteland for the uncaring, Rafi had worked out a system for loners: arrived home at twelve thirty in the morning, had a banana and tea, and stretched out on the fraying couch to read the latest installment of the *Library for Random Wisdom* pamphlet series, distributed weekly by mail to subscribers. It had saved his sanity. Some of it was advice, "Your daring is the answer." Plus, there was something from that guy Nietzsche, who kept popping in almost all the issues, "He who has a WHY to live can bear almost any HOW." Rafi likes this.

A savior, a floating plank in this raging sea of loneliness and despair, Rafi wanted a why to live and was ready to fight for it. There was no question that he would dare this time.

He was developing a complete personal philosophy. Starting after midnight, at the brink of a new day, illuminated by his conscience's needs. Wherever this took him, the happiness of being alive was the greatest accomplishment. He went on and on thinking thus. He worried it was a bit crazy. He looked around, pretending he was awakening from a dream that had brought him to unfamiliar surroundings.

The room was familiar all right, but he cringed from the sight: dusty, plain, dejected, and lacking any sense of aesthetics. What had he been thinking all these years? Nothing that he could consider now to be a solid foundation. He was stuck in feelings of the past, an inner space of poverty, where the possibilities of the present didn't count, were irrelevant. He was living like a laborer without a skill or knowledge, without a vision. Thinking this last thought hurt.

Renata was on his mind. That is all, besides the desolation in which he lived. He could not invite her here. He had to change the way this looked now: clean the place, move somewhere, buy some flowers. Desperation assaulted him: Did he resemble his room? Did he smell like it? How could anyone love him then?

Wait. Use your philosophy, Rafi. You have lived here for three good years. It's true the walls have the look of puke after you had one beer too many. But you can paint. There are real things to think about, your long-lived loneliness. You've been silent so long that you don't know the sound of your own voice. It is true that you come across as … different. Plus, the memory of your mother's accent. You break the mold. But others are doing the same. Go find them.

Thinking, stretched on the stiff couch that had put up with him every night since he started in the local police force, Rafi felt an unknown sense of peacefulness embrace his arms and legs, inviting a smile to play over his face. *Peace* was what the calm woman had said to him. She didn't expect a response, perhaps. Living in that street of hers, what could she expect from anyone?

Sueña despierto, y volarás … Dream awake, and you'll fly. How he had dismissed those words from his grandmother as nonsense! She was an old woman from another country where things go slow. Here, where he lived, one should not dream, just go fast, big, and calculate. Move. Go, even if you don't know where or why or even believe in anything. He remembered the words vividly, as if he had just awakened from a deep slumber, and said them aloud in Spanish—a recovered memory indicating a path, a song to the heart. He remembered them because he was ready to understand. He had started to move on from a state of indifference and emptiness to one of caring.

Gracias, abuela.

PAULI

THIRTY

RENATA TAKES THE TRAIN

The idea of taking the train to New Brook opened the door to possible resolutions, as all inquiries should. Abandoning oneself to understanding was the scariest of moments, as it left the old self behind. There was no going back. One might get afraid and refuse to take all due steps to liberation, but life won't be the same. One would never be the same. That innocence was gone, and its memory would look down on you, slipping into your consciousness the identity of the failure.

It would have been impossible to imagine, just the day before, what she was about to do now, or even know then that it was necessary. But here she was, Renata, on the first day of February, buying a round-trip ticket to New Brook, to the organic coffee shop with Wi-Fi by the train station, just to check on whether the quantum realm bullies could trace her during the trip, while having coffee around people with internet connection, and she without her phone.

Or she could find out if now the people oppressing her were of a different kind altogether, as the stalkers of two days ago suggested--- "paid stalkers."

The night of January 30, she was leaving the downtown Latino restaurant where she had ordered chips and coffee to pass time away from the Sotos.

And that afternoon, the day before her first court appearance, It, the Old Goat, had been especially aggressive. Could he be following a plan designed by the evil son, to try to tire Renata out, to force her to give up, to break her down? Even with her prayers for protection clamoring all over the house, plus the holy potion to drive out evil made from common water and castile soap, the budget and charity counselor ghost reigned in her home, unseen. He gloated in his power, his insincere religious faith forgotten.

When Renata went up to the attic to take refuge in her futon and the fiend came in no time to snuggle up to her belly, giggling with all this fun, Renata broke into tears. She ran downstairs and into the bathroom, sensing she would vomit, but all her body wanted to get rid of was the sorrow this evil jerk was bringing to her existence.

How could she have been so abandoned? What was the meaning of this random pouring of darkness? Why had the universe written this strange fate for her? Could she change anything? She ran to the living room table, sat down, and put her head on the tablecloth, crying as if there were no consolation left in the Universe. Even when she was a child, pushed around by hardened siblings and a brutalized father, Renata had not wept with such conviction. Sobs like waves or prayers burst from her belly and took refuge in her breasts, Embrace's Cradle. And there, in that terrible present, Renata wept. The sobs came to her breast, and she uttered their verse again and again. Crying is the beginning of a resolution. She had gone back to the bathroom for a towel, and there was the stupid ghost of the fake counselor, saying *Oh, Oh, Oh!*

Outside, she could hear Hubber coming out of his basement and standing by the fence. Renata didn't know whether he would help with this. She had texted to him to please tell the authorities how the invisibility works, not to speak against anyone, but because it was the duty of a citizen of a democratic society. Hubber had not responded, afraid maybe of his possible implication.

Renata got her bag and left the house for the library to do some thinking, without the Soto ghost touching her breasts and pushing her around in the hallway. The intensity of the horrible monster's actions implied a plan to drive her crazy before the court appearance, to tire her out, to make her forget her duty, to give up. A gang's point of view.

From the library, she tried to figure out where to get a space to sit out the night. She texted Jill Justin of the NAACP. Such prompt response! She sent the homeless shelter phone, where she knew she was not welcome, because she had a home. Safe Futures said the same as before. This was not a domestic dispute. Jill kept texting. She wrote that she was going to contact a friendly policeman.

He called and said, "We can come and escort you to your home."

"And why would you do that? Aren't you hearing that I am fleeing my home because I am abused by the neighbor?"

"Have you reported this to the police, ma'am?"

"Yes. Many times."

"And what did they say?"

"I was arrested. Tomorrow, I have a court date because of the police."

"Well, what can I do?"

"Stay away from my home. Do not ever go there again."

And Renata hung up. She looked at her phone and saw that Jill was not texting anymore. Renata sent a message, saying that being escorted by the police just suggested she was in more trouble. But Jill had disappeared. The library would close at seven, in about twenty minutes.

Homeless for the night, and tomorrow having to be at the courthouse at nine. Renata thought of the Mexican restaurant, La Cocina, open until one in the morning, where she could be safe for an hour or two. She didn't know at this time that her car was being tracked down, but she will start understanding as the night, the day, the next night, and the day progressed.

When she came out of La Cocina at nine, closing time on Mondays, the same white van that followed her to the supermarket in the morning, the same one which found her after she tried to lose it and then started the engine loudly as she came out of the store, the same that was starting the engine loudly now as she left the downtown restaurant. Exactly. It was a scaring technique from the underworld.

Renata bought a hat and a scarf at the dollar store and a bag of peanuts. It was dark enough now for her to go home on the sly and get a blanket. With luck, she could spend a quiet night inside the emergency room parking lot at the hospital, moving around to fool the security car. She did get two hours of rest there on Friday night, essential for functioning. When she got near the house, she parked down by the apartments and walked. Opening her door and awakening the Old Goat was one essential moment in the Terror of Eternity, like in the tales of childhood abandoned. The Old Goat, the senile counselor, was the ogre of folklore and memory and of the unstudied future. He growled in the night while Renata escaped with her golden and red throw down the hill and ran away in her car.

She discarded the idea of playing hide-and-seek with security by the emergency room. Besides, she needed respect. She wanted respect. With just her purse with two bananas inside, a notebook, and a bottle of water, Renata entered the empty hospital entrance room, full of fancy benches hardly anybody ever sat on, on their way to visit the dying, to bring home the destined to return. But the seats were necessary for the living, for those passing by, in hope and sorrow, as through a forest of trials, mystery, and the familiar.

Renata asked for permission to sit on one of the small benches. The security guard looked at her quizzically, and Renata, not knowing it was prohibited, said she wanted to sit there in memory of her uncle, who stayed at the hospital at the end of his life. It wasn't the real reason, but with the truth, she couldn't get anything anywhere.

Meeting joy lasts but a second, and Renata felt cared for and included in the safety plan of the city, or at least of the hospital, for a moment. The security guard understood her need for healing, and they talked about in-house counselors Renata may want to contact in the morning. She gave him one of her bananas.

Soon, there was a change of guard for the night, and Renata heard the difficulties of the working class juggling multiple schedules while caring for sick relatives and arriving late to the graveyard shift—from the safety of her bench, where she was writing one more chapter of the story she was living. But writing was a happy occupation, even if the subject were her own sorrow.

"Ms., how long ago did your uncle pass away?"

"Two years."

It wasn't true; it was more like three and a few months, but it didn't look bad to be mourning after two years, a bit suspicious after three years, and making it all the way to the waiting room in the hospital in the wee hours of the morning just for that.

"Well now, you rest there with your diary. It will be all right."

"Thank you. If you have a family, you know what this is."

"I have a family all right."

"Are you married?"

"My fiancée wants to get married in 2026."

"Why wait so long? You never know what will happen. Don't waste time!"

"Well, she wants to have that big wedding! You know, by the beach with friends and a big buffet, a fancy dress, and whatnot. All that costs money."

"Wow! Does she want to have children?"

"Oh, yes. We already have two, and one is on the way."

"Well, in that case, I am sure that wedding can wait. Good luck to you."

And the groom-to-be smiled but walked around looking at the floor, a bit bent with responsibilities that at that time of the night, in his third part-time job of the day, didn't seem that necessary. Soon, the real full-time security of the hospital came around and asked questions about Renata. The man explained the best he could, since he had not been the one who had allowed her to sit there.

But Renata was thinking that moving again would be the thing to do. She had sensed the thin wiretapping on her hair already, and her legs were being visited by the heavy energy that said the monster-counselor had located her once again.

She told the security man that she was wrapping up her diary entry, which had been really healing, she added, and would return home to rest. The man heaved a sigh of relief. He didn't want any conflict with the hospital; it was an easy job, and he had that promise given to that girlfriend mother of his children...

As she left the main space of the waiting room, where the hospital stored the wheelchairs to bring patients in and out, a shadow came out from behind those wheelchairs and looked at Renata fixedly while smoking a cigarette, puffing with rage. A young Latino: he looked poor, hair to his shoulders, emaciated, in second-hand tight clothes. The Old Goat or the son probably hired him. He was maybe somebody who came to the church to feel welcome someplace, or a small-time criminal who got cash or dope for jobs like this one. He followed Renata to her car, threw away the cigarette with disdain, and left the hospital grounds walking.

It was close to two in the morning. She had to be at the courthouse by nine, and the mayor's assistant had advised her to go at eight thirty to talk to the prosecutor, so Justice would have the necessary background to deal with the case. She arrived home, and without any lights on, she stretched out on the little cot she had assembled in the old bedroom, to be safer. The Old Goat was laying on top of her, right away, in his teleportation energy, all four hundred pounds of him. She got up.

It was clear that there was a plot to make her useless at the courthouse, maybe even miss the appointment, which meant she would have to pay $1,000. The servants of Satan from the famous counseling joint had it all figured out. This ghetto brotherhood had given them something of what they wanted. Not all, though. Hardly anything, really. Even with the house with the yard and the big swollen cars, they looked poor. Renata took a big blanket and sat on the porch outside, the house lights on. Out there, there was little magnetic presence of the Ghoul, such as the feeling that he wanted to hang on to her back. Soon it disappeared.

Around three thirty, she came in and sat at the living room table to type what she redacted at the hospital, some of the most beautiful two pages she had ever written. Despite the loneliness of the woman in the story, there was happiness, gentleness, and even some kind of love: Pauli the Ghost, the beautiful spirit that loved her for a while. Language was such a consolation, a guide! What would she have done if she didn't have this skill, this gift of the spirit? Now she understood those who take justice into their own hands and do the violent action required to set their world in order. But she was one of the chosen few, who could write and dialogue with the memory of the experiences, and summon them from sleep for reflection, happiness, and even some kind of justice.

This is what she wrote in her notebook by hand at the hospital waiting room, and at home on her laptop in the wee hours, to be safe in writing, to avoid the Old Goat's abuse.

Pauli, the Lovable Ghost
A Meditation on Beauty and Gentleness

She returned home in peace, yearning for a better life there. Renata had reported the Sotos, and she was looking forward to a peaceful neighborhood. There was an unfamiliar emptiness in her: not sadness but readiness. Like a room, aired and painted, space for welcoming the whispers of the world, this mysterious place was where we travel while searching for our essence.

The Sotos had dispersed, and as if their souls suspected they were being found out, a hush tightened their house like a gag. But they were not learning; their world was already settled within the stifling dealings of the tribe, just waiting out for danger to pass, and following their program for dragging Renata away. Renata was not important to the law, and they could outsmart it anyhow with the help of their tricks and connections.

Renata looked out of the attic window, and new tinted security windows faced her, silent, watchful, and maybe afraid. Again, as she had done in the past, she wondered whether Hubber could be an ally. It was a stupid thought really because he had been such an unfriendly neighbor almost from the start, when Betty recruited him for the neighborhood bully plan, and so rejecting her so brutally. She knew he was just following the bully culture as a way of being accepted. Maybe now he would be able to change, if the Sotos stepped back. He had done many things, like coming up in the middle of the night up her porch and touching the screen of the window where she slept, something that suggested he wanted to connect but didn't know how.

Without having thought it through, she exclaimed, "Hubber!"

She sensed he had heard. But that was all that answered her, the feeling he was listening to her by his computer, aware of her.

Exhausted due to the sleepless hours of harassment by the Sotos, Renata turned off the stick lamplight by the futon. As she touched the pillow, an embrace of warmth and what could be considered care rolled onto her shoulder, across the room from

Hubber's window. It stayed, not static like a thing but evolving like life, an emotion, a gift presented, a need, following with heart steps that wanted a resolution.

Renata felt happy. There was nobody with her, just this energy, this ghost, that Pauli Ghost she had pretended to know so much about, something that scared Hubber and kept his friends away from experiment parties after she hung two oversized male underwear on the fence between the two houses with a message. It read, "Dear Pauli Principle Ghost: did you leave this behind last night in the house where you went to fart? Happy New Year."

Renata sensed his fear. She was into something. And he didn't want the secret outside of the circle of friends, which maybe included Soto Jr., who had probably taught others.

There was nobody there with her, although it wasn't true. A cool breath came close to her face, and hands that were not hands caressed the hills of her breasts like a skilled mountaineer who loves every step and sight and for whom it's more of a joy to retrace the way than to get to the top fast.

Pauli the Ghost moved like an accomplished lover, reaching the left side of the futon with an agility that suggested not only a light frame in his everyday material life but a calculation of the distance of his targets exactly to the nano-millimeter.

Pauli caressed Renata in her flesh from the consciousness of his own desire. He didn't seem to need a finite body to understand pleasure.

Renata felt he may have studied anatomy with angels, so knowledgeable Pauli the Ghost was about something so human---and also gentle, thoughtful, and passionate, with that enviable softness of ethereal beings that can be in two places at the same time and manage with poise and authority the realities of more than one dimension.

Most likely, Pauli had learned all this exquisite loving with real bodies and as a real body himself, bodies he was not afraid of, younger men at college and the military academy, tender, willing, virginal, and pure in intent, without ties or future.

The present ... deep ... satisfactory ... forever.

This didn't mean that he would not return, just that he didn't have to. Renata most likely would think he was a product of her dream state, the space between the oppression of our days and the liberty of eternity.

Pauli the Ghost knew of certain kind of love but had no heart to place over Renata's beating one and thus ground a union of souls.

Anything like a memory of him could be ascribed to the realm of Einstein's famous "Spooky action in the distance" phrase, except now it was near and there was nobody to guide anyone in the understanding of what to do. And this oversight by the official side of science was terrible because it left the whole world at the mercy of the unethical.

But back to the event and its vocabulary: with the elegant authority of the master, Pauli the Ghost caressed his way down Renata's body to the belly button, not mechanical at all. His thing, felt Renata, was design. She felt the discipline of the form, its meaning, the feeling it awoke. It was a physical sensation, a movement of beauty like a dance, something of accomplishment, something of substance for memory's hunger. But who says that the awakening of pleasure is not the meaning of life? A well-conceived circle around the belly button, where life begins, deep, probing, pitiless, sincere, revised thoroughly again.

By Renata's left arm, an added artery pumped, fresh and laborious, as if Pauli could bring himself to breathe for the occasion. To be, finally! To take responsibility for the moment, lying down next to the woman he had betrayed, as if waiting for a sealing kiss.

But Renata was happy. She stretched on the futon, knowing Pauli the Ghost was next to her, although not daring to look at him, at whatever Pauli was. She went down to the bathroom and wondered whether he would take a shower here in the morning or cross the two walls of their houses and vanish, the way he came.

All felt new, the bedcover and her shirt, the way the moonlight fell through the skylight by the foot of the bed, the thought of breakfast in the morning. The pumping sounds by her left arm were a little less vital, mostly empty. Sleep was coming over Renata, thinking of breakfast and that shower, and the how of it all. She fell asleep, blossoming like a sidereal bride.

Renata fixed coffee and two boiled eggs and ate, attentive to the Goat's energy around the bathroom, to take a furtive shower in the dark if he were on nap time. The resistance to this cowardly persecution gave Renata an air of authority and strength, as if she just came from a rejuvenating vacation. She dressed up, new shoes dusted; navy-blue pants, ironed; a cashmere red cardigan; a camel-color pea coat taken out of the plastic in which it had been wrapped since the cleaners returned it, adorned with her pin as teacher of the National Junior Thespian Association.

Renata could act, and this morning, she was a bossy snob, a well-off professional, a woman going places. She stopped by the DD near the courthouse, and she could smell the respect from the women serving coffee from the first step into the shop, teeming with less lucky individuals.

"Everything bagel, toasted, no butter," Renata gave the order with conviction.

And the woman server knew exactly what she wanted and examined the new client with interest, as if wanting to memorize the color combination as a reference for her own important occasion. Munching the bread carefully, to not to spoil her appearance with crumbs, Renata reviewed the notes she carefully had developed at home, to share with the prosecutor, for all to know what the situation was and thus work together toward a solution.

"They will wipe clean your record since you have no antecedents."

That's what the mayor's assistant had said. She complained of unbearable abuse, and they made a criminal out of her, letting the real ones on the loose, and respectable. Her notes were as aseptic as she could make them, with no passion, just the facts as clear and logically ordered as she could make them, so as not to give them the opportunity of saying, "That's crazy. You are making things up." They had to believe her.

Snow flurries had been coming down since dawn, but now, as the Superior Court was about to open, the only thing left was a wet sidewalk, erratic, thick raindrops, and an oppressive grayness over this world. A sad man, chunky and in distress, waited for the opening of the court building, hunched over the wheel of his running SUV.

"They'll open it soon."

He went back to his worrying, his brooding. Sadness was refuge and consolation; sadness was the only kind emotion one had left. What could one do for the powerless, the silent ones? She, Renata, had the advice of City Hall. She had Dup, the private investigator, who sat across from her house on a frigid night at a time when all the nights were warm, to see if anyone would enter her house, although she had a camera there, and the question was the intrusion of ghosts. She didn't blame him. Who could believe this? Of course, Dup shouldn't take advantage. And he had.

Renata had a duty from her privileged position, to stick to her guns. Justice must be honored. Even in this strange-effects quantum realm, justice had a place. And if her story had happened to one of these people summoned to the Superior Court today, she or he would have been destroyed, driven away, called crazy, and worse. Renata could not leave them alone. More than ever now, she had to fight this, to find a way to tell the truth on behalf of those who couldn't.

When Renata entered the building and gave her bag to the guard, he looked at her, like saying, "You are using the wrong door. This here is where we let the criminals in." But she insisted he keep her umbrella. She was going to court as a criminal. She asked where the prosecutor's office was. She was never really answered either by the guard at the door or the one inside the courtroom. There was no meeting with the prosecutor ahead of the hearing. Just write your name and sit down. She wrote her name first. Then the others did, and they all sat there in public court, like in the public square hangings of old. What was the mayor's assistant thinking of? Had not the poor descended in the scale of rights, the scale of the convenient?

"Do you have an attorney?"

The prosecutor looked like a distressed high school senior, overweight and wearing the same T-shirt for which no boy would ever ask her out to the senior dance. She must be wondering why Renata was there, whether she herself knew.

"If you don't, and so that you know, you have to pay eight hundred dollars for damages."

"What?"

"Yes, there is an invoice for car damages."

"I never knew that. Damages of what?"

"You have until March 4 to figure this out. You may leave."

Renata stopped by the mayor's office on the way home.

"The problem is that you don't get along with the neighbors!" This was the assistant to the mayor, who could not accept the fact that he knew nothing about prosecutors.

"Can you, or they, say exactly what I do? They are the ones who trespass, yell, leave trash on my doorstep, and break my locks. You must know yourself, a colored man, what racism or bigotry looks like. Don't you? Why must the victim be blamed?"

The assistant cooled down. Not being well educated in the law, not even in community issues or on the new trends on matters of bigotry, he thought sometimes that just acting tough would finally convince Renata that she should look at her own actions to explain all this mess.

"Well, they accuse you of criminal mischief."

"Because I left a note telling them to stop harassing me. But this bill is an inside job. Fraudulent. They didn't arrest me for damaging anything. They are mixing stories on purpose."

"You can't prove."

"I could prove, if you listen, that Soto Jr. has inside help bringing his car bill through the police and inside the state court system for me to pay something that is his responsibility. Do you know how many felonies he has committed, just with this act? I have given enough information about what they do. There are even some videos, lots of photos of the damage. Even the firemen called the police when they fixed my broken lock, arguing there was a serious concern. But nothing of this count."

"All right. Tell Dup about it. He may have some advice."

Coming home early from the court date seemed to Renata like such a perfect thing to do, being innocent in the courtroom sense and especially after a night without sleep, thanks to the Sotos and their thugs about town. But one wouldn't think that way if the person had lived in the ghetto before. The snowy raindrops had stopped, and although the day looked sad, nothing announced difficulty. The Soto's house was quiet, and Jr.'s car was there, as if all had gathered for a slumber party after the animated evening and dawn.

She made tea, brought it up to the attic, and stretched out on the futon with Baldwin's *Another Country* from the newly organized Urban Literature section at the library. The young assistants, who came with loads of enthusiasm and never stayed, kept the old space updated and young in certain places.

She thought she should get a pad and write down the fantastic line, "… he had received the blow from which he never would recover, and this nobody wanted to believe."

Renata fell asleep. AnnaLynn, the Soto woman, the same one Renata reported to the police days before for being in her bedroom through whatever gadget inside her bedroom one morning at four---came now in a virtual manner by the open book and mumbled nonsense utterings.

Renata woke up. How did they know she was falling asleep? She had asked herself this many times before. She thought there was a camera or the invisible man, always popping in, knew somehow. But she was too tired to ask any more questions. For how long had she not been allowed to sleep longer than two hours? Really, her only strength was her resiliency. Any answers, insights, and even facts were no proof as far as the police were concerned. If only she could stay strong and say no to the insistence of evil, opposing the indecency of their behavior, their lack of democracy.

Listening to her tarot spread for the week was a better choice than the book. She could close her eyes while getting the message. The white feather tarot was always so inspiring. Choosing a card and a stone over the others and hearing the soothing voice speaking to you so convincingly about how your future, the possibility of coming out a winner over any obstacles, was the best way to wake up any day.

Renata fell asleep again. It could have been around noon. She was trying to go to sleep for about one hour, one hour and a half. And now, she was awakened for the second time.

The white feather tarot was still giving advice in the distance; the laptop had fallen over to one side. But over her belly, there was the awareness of another belly, not a real body but an alternative reality one, a strange quantum effect belly, the spooky action of Einstein, no longer at a distance, but here, at the service of evil and unethical minds. It was Soto's son, his bare belly being communicated with somehow; he moaned with pleasure, the pleasure of spoiling a hated person's nap while masturbating.

It was a family reunion. They didn't get the $800 they thought they would get from Renata, with the help of the phony invoice from a friend's garage. But they would get that money. All they had to do was wear her out until she couldn't think anymore. They would get that money. All was planned.

She did that afternoon what she had done all the other times when they didn't let her rest. Renata went downstairs to the old bedroom, her big cushions-and-blankets-on-the-rug movie refuge. She shook the big comforter in the middle of the room and spread the cushions. It was very cozy there.

As soon as Renata rested her head on the pillows, an excited voice came from under the cover, and the awareness of strong arms hugging her middle under the breasts, as if wanting to explode her lungs, made Renata get up instantly. The Old Goat was here, waiting for her.

Renata realized she could not fight this alone. If she stayed in the house, the ghosts would be pushing her shoulders, touching her genitals, hanging over her, and breathing hard when she used the toilet, getting inside the covers where she was, squeezing her lungs until she couldn't breathe, acting out long-distance electric shocks to her heart, her back, arm, and mouth, all the while pretending to act out all imaginable indignities. Probably they were doing them for real, wherever they were. Unimaginable as all this was, it was happening nearby.

She called the Salvation Army in town, a place where she had gone sometimes for breakfast, invited by the directors because she could speak Spanish. The wife took the message and said someone would call her soon. Although their programs were limited, they would see what could be done. Something always could be done.

And this changed everything for Renata. That something, this always, that could be done. Soon the woman called back, saying that her husband, Major Brian, was on his way to the hotel across the street and to come with ID anytime now. All was ready for her to have a safe space. There was no talk of Renata paying for her room. This was their service to the community. Whatever was not in place due to scarce resources, they made up for it by providing for the present need and setting a precedent for the community to know how to act.

Of course, Renata was to understand much later. The fact that Old Goat located her in her hotel room later that afternoon was no mystery. They were listening to her conversation. She had forgotten in her distress that she knew her cell phone was bugged from the Soto's dark den.

January 22

Last night, I slept at Fred's. Before I went away from the house, the Old Goat followed me with his ghost instrument, blowing on my face, sticking close to my body, and trying to touch my breast. He followed me to my basement and didn't go into the garden. But I could sense the energy, waiting, keeping very close to my butt. I left about four thirty.

He found me in the other house around midnight. He tried to stretch on my back, but I pushed him out. I returned home this morning around ten thirty and took a shower before he found me again, which he did soon. In the afternoon, I went to the library, and he showed up there too, patting my legs up to my butt with his electronic equipment, his GPS, whatever allows him to be a long-distance criminal, secret, and without danger to himself. The greatest irresponsibility.

THIRTY-ONE

TESTIMONY FROM RAFI SALCEDO

We agreed to meet, I, as a civilian friend, at the library on Saturday morning of that interesting week. We had bumped into one another at the police station. She went in to fill in a complaint, and I was going out on my beat. She seemed upbeat, full of energy, following her intuition of what she must do to protect and defend herself. *Defend* is the word needed here.

This is so different from all the other cases we had, that, at least for me, it was a joy to talk to her about how this neighborhood thing was developing. My colleagues, ah, well, there were all kinds of opinions, although some were beginning to feel for her. The situation was dragging on, and no one took her seriously. For me, she was consistent. She could not be inventing this awful story. If we didn't listen, too bad for us. We were failing to learn something new. And if the thing were true, we were not protecting, certainly not serving the innocent.

So that morning of February 1, the day after her memorable court appearance on a charge that didn't exist because there was nothing presented to the court to go on, just that fraudulent bill from the Sotos, she came to the station to report what had happened at the hotel where she spent the night, a guest of the Salvation Army social services. She stopped by the senior center first, where the city's Human Services were, to see whether they would help her report it to the state police, but it was closed for some reason. She then called Major Brian to see what she should do because we, her town's police, were no longer on her list of people or whatever you want to call this. Only because Major Brian asked her to report it, she showed up and bumped into me.

One important detail of that call to Major Brian was that she now knew for sure that her phone was bugged. When Major Brian said, "They are following you through your phone," and Renata said, "No way, my phone is just a phone. I can't get my emails there," the gang, probably Old Soto or AnnaLynn, clicked twice to let her know that they heard her opinion. But Brian wanted her to report the event, and she did it, explaining that she was following sort of orders from her benefactor, who had paid for a room for her at the hotel next door because she was unsafe in her house.

The policeman, who had been in her house once, said that story about hearing voices meant to him that she should be checked by the doctors. She told me that she had answered, "You have a right to your opinion, Officer, but we are here to report facts. I don't hear voices. I hear the voice of the person doing the harassment. What's the number for this?"

The officer was told through the speaker that there was no number. And she insisted on having a number. She reported that Old Soto had appeared in his bodiless/out-of-body travel persona at her hotel room, once at night and the other when she was in the bathroom in the morning, and the thing had to be done well. The police were being selective here; they didn't keep any of her reports of Old Soto. For some reason, his name was not written on the space for the accused. This was very perceptive of her. She was on to something. They gave her a number for her visit, though. Why didn't they do some basic research on what she was saying?

I don't think anybody wanted to know what Soto Jr. was really doing. Friends with the Chief and Captain Caballero. It's too scary, even for me. I don't want to know. If this were not my job, I wouldn't want to look this deep into the darkness of the soul. That's the real horror, not the plastic monsters in movies.

She was giving us an essential fact disclosed later by the researchers of symptoms of electronic harassment: that victims can hear their abusers talking and so they can be identified if they are acquaintances.

The month of January into February was intense. Everyone revealed his true self. The police somehow accepted this phony Soto's invoice, protecting the gang, which vandalized her car every time she didn't pay and was let go by the Judge at the Courthouse. The old man took this as a go-ahead and accosted Renata day and night, even when outside of her home: at the library, tracking her down on her walks, at the dentist, at the choir rehearsal, even out of town.

The other neighbors, the original bullies, hoped Renata would be driven out somehow, but this time they didn't want to be involved. Something dangerous was going on. It made them quiet. They were so afraid of becoming the victims of the invisible thing.

Renata gave her cell to Major Brian, to test if it was the phone what allowed her abusers to track her and left for the grocery store. She was free for about ten minutes. Then she felt something of the weight, figuratively speaking, something of the ample figure of the counselor making a presence in her car, very near to her, as she drove to buy snacks for this day of investigation. The bodiless ghost, the hounding energy, pushed Renata from side to side inside the car, as if wishing her to have an accident.

In the store, she was free again, and this could mean that her car was being tracked, probably. Moving very quickly, she approached all the people she could see using cell phones. She would ask associates where something was—she perfectly knew where it was—just so they would walk with her for a while with their own wireless identity. Renata had figured out how to be tracked-free!

And then she came to check out. And there she understood why Soto Jr. was wearing a strip over his mouth on the afternoon of the second Sunday of the year, the weekend of the virtual rape by both Sotos at the same time. It was to read her mouth's signals, to add to her biometric identity profile. The people tracking her had quite an organization. And all for what? What did they want to know? There was no reason other than that she didn't submit to a tribal system, where nothing of growth or beauty was allowed.

As she opened her car, a strong magnetic force, like the one she had suffered at home around her ribs, under her chest, hugged her feet violently. But it didn't make her fall. She was being so careful. Renata had not thought yet this could be *brujo* energy. It felt to her like the counselor was enraged she had escaped. Now, after seeing that he could come in his magnetic-wave self into the hotel room and follow her to the supermarket even without her phone, what would happen if Renata left town? This was the information she had intended to get for the state police. This guy could inflict harm from his den in other parts of the state, not just in Old Yantic.

Away from her house, her phone, and her car—those objects, rituals, chores, and duties we call life, as lived up to this moment—Renata felt like the group of homeless that pretended to be going someplace while hanging out at the train station. Moving seats, going out to bum a cigarette, coming back, and continuing a story that was no story--- just words and pretense to support them in the passing of time. She was a little bit like them. She didn't need to bum anything because she could pay. But the peace she had at home, her privacy, had been destroyed, taken away by this brute, with the help of some gadget or computer program, voodoo-like black magic, the help of his family, of revenge tricks learned in a life of penury and discrimination. These homeless had been pushed out of where they used to belong by blind poverty, ignorance, an inflexible system that could not use them. But why was she being pushed out? Why this insistence on accosting her by way of this invisible perfect-crime trick?

She took the train to the organic coffee shop at New Brook shopping center, bought one of their long-sleeve shirts, had coffee, and ate from the bag of shelled peanuts she had brought, waiting for the next train back. Yes, forty minutes after she had arrived, the extreme cold air hugged her legs, and the metallic wiretapping on the head was there. They had a good system, a useless system to pass their time, like the homeless at the train station, but with an objective, harming somebody's life.

The question now for Renata was how to recover her private space, denounce the gang, and discourage fascism, the disrespect for the other. Everything was against her. Even if anyone believed her, no one dared to say. It was too bizarre. But the authorities would surely be concerned with this, with the terrible social implications of this technology in the hands of perverts, organized gangs, and crooks. She was on to something relevant to peace.

Her cell phone was still at Major Brian's; her car was at the library. She would return home when it got dark and take the train early to Great Green, to the regional FBI offices. Renata knew that tracking people by individuals, the nastiest form of stalking, was illegal, much more illegal if they were so well equipped that their team, whatever that meant, could do it across cities, rivers, or the state, an hour and fifteen minutes by train. She would find out soon enough.

She was received at home that night by the same cold air around the feet as in the coffee shop across the river, thirty minutes away by train. When she put her head on the pillow, the counselor's voice was heard, clear and nasty, menacing, "Up there!" as if Renata being in her own home were of public interest at ten in the evening.

And then early, around five in the morning, the fetid electric air blew mercilessly on her face. She put a pillow over to cover her nose. Then the pressure around her thorax made it impossible to stay stretched out; she sat up in time to reject once more the prowling around her pubic area that had become so present since the counselor had started making his way into her house nightly, daily, infinitely. She would take the train again, a longer ride. Somebody had to understand.

At the train station early in the morning, waiting next to the homeless who use the room around the clock, her head was tapped again, and Old Soto snooped on her until the train departed. What a joy, to be free, taken away from this hell by the train. Just you, the common air, the sky, the birds, and the others, quietly sitting by your side, smiling if they can, or nursing their own grief. Just being.

In Great Green, Renata went into the organic grocery, Green City Market, for a cup of coffee and to freshen up. She had been there ten minutes roughly when she went to brush her teeth, and as she started to comb her hair, the fetid air blew on her face. The heavy magnetic presence followed her as she paid and walked into the sunny day, following with intent the numbers written on each building, next to the sidewalk on the busy street, near the big highway. She wondered whether the neighbors could see her now from their dark den in the hometown. Renata, so grown up in the city, was afraid that the authorities this time wouldn't believe her.

When Renata stopped at the FBI headquarters, a young man of the type that had been following her, without a known profession, an expensive cell phone by his ear, and inexpressive eyes on her, settled by a window on the building across the street. Without emotion, he stared. Renata gave her identification to the guard, who let her in and asked her to sit down while a female interrogator came to see her.

The woman, wearing a shirt from Q. University in a nearby town, was pleasant. She was not well informed but a good listener. Renata was winning her heart when the listening device taping her was turned off. Soon after, the guard came out and announced the interview was over and gave Renata her laptop, telling her that its contents had been copied.

"Then you have part of my late uncle's biography for your reading pleasure."

The man seemed taken aback, and the woman looked sorry. But Renata left in a good mood. If they decide to investigate, it would be a good day for women's safety, for freedom. If they followed the police advice, which probably they were doing when they copied her laptop, then Renata was alone with her struggle.

When she returned home, she understood that the Sotos knew where she had been. The following day, the bamboo she had placed under a fence in the back of the garden with a wide space under had been removed, and her composter lid was moved halfway. She noticed bits and pieces from the slops, placed on the lid. It sported half a banana skin, half an eggshell, and a handful of soil over the composter lid, carefully arranged, footprints left by the discontented invisible abusers. They wanted her to know they were watching.

The Sotos would wait for a few days, slamming doors on her, farting next to her window in the middle of the night, and bringing the gang to destroy the paint on her car's hood. And if nothing happened, they'd continue as usual, nastier and oftener with more involved, like AnnaLynn, who was now in charge of bringing her magnetic presence to Renata's bed while masturbating and calling Renata's name.

Renata got up and left her room. It was before six in the morning. She couldn't even wake up in peace. You can say, "Sure, others wake up to bombs. What's the problem? This is a dangerous world."

The problem is that she is being targeted by people considered decent and protected by the police, but who are involved in dangerous and illegal activity. Those throwing bombs do what they do in the open, risking all. These criminals go to their church on Sunday and do the counseling stuff for a few hours and get paid more than most in a month.

And we are silent. What does it say about us? One of those nights around the court appearance, Renata called a former student of her uncle's, a near neighbor, well-connected to the party, with power, if anyone around here has any. She had been on committees, brought into the council to fill a vacant seat. She listened and thought that everything would be all right. Just go home and listen to music. Really. Why is it difficult to understand what's truly happening?

Renata started talking, and this woman's husband went to bed without any interest in the fact that she felt unsafe in her own home. Although the woman said she felt disappointed in the mayor and the chief of police, she didn't contact them and said, "Look, pay attention to this, or I will start a group to guide women in this situation." She had been on the board of the women's center, and now she could give no help. That should tell you something about the quality of the engagement. They show up to protest when it is politically correct, when it is safe to bring flowers for the dead. But when an action or well-directed words could have saved a life, that's missing. It's the culture of the absent. We are so specialized that soon we'll have nothing useful for anyone, nothing in common to connect us.

This woman, for what it's worth, was suggesting something reasonable, that a plan be implemented and checked periodically to see if it worked, to make clear what was expected of everyone, like stopping what they were doing that was harmful to others, and to involve the River Guard Institute and Hubber's supervisor, to see whether he had introduced any scientific experimentation and practices in the neighborhood that had changed the face of harassment essentially.

Renata said that a curtain was left lifted where she had placed plastic for safety. This was the Old Goat's mark. They could get into the house, and you couldn't see them. They were there, day and night, touching your behind with their invisible hands. Renata's friend said that it looked like some military secret had leaked out and all were afraid of saying anything. But Renata was beginning to suspect it was something primitive, much older than recorded by modern science.

It was, really, the perfect crime. Probably the original bullies didn't really know about what the Sotos had introduced for harassment and control. But they sensed something unholy going on, dark and nasty, and withdrew somewhat. They wanted Renata to get harmed, but not themselves. And besides, they were afraid now that their own story of harassment, which had been taken over by the underworld, was pushing them out of any fun they could have had, if only they had been let in the secret.

That neighborhood's important woman also said that Hubber Dixon, the guy who never spoke to Renata after being inducted into the bullies' club, should be brought into the conversations. But I guess that contacting the River Institute was not politically advisable because the politicians wanted to be on good term with them, the bigger guys.

There is always a bigger guy, especially in small places like this. The city didn't even ignore the suggestion. As far as they were concerned, the police and anyone else, the terrible thing was not happening. I'm telling this to show the intelligence and daring that Renata never hid, even in this terrible situation.

One day, the assistant to the mayor said something like, "That's unbelievable. You don't see the guys who come into your house, and you think we are so gullible as to believe the story!"

Renata said she realized there was something mischievous about her. She took the opportunity to put the jerk in his place. "Do you believe in God or at least in the angels?"

"Sure, why wouldn't I believe in them? We all believe. Most of us, at least."

"Have you ever seen them?"

The guy gave up. He didn't give a damn about what she was saying, but she did have an art with language. And she also had a point. There could be some mysterious wireless gadget he had never heard about doing this thing she said they were doing. He kept a door open for her. It was a good policy, sort of politically correct in some manner or another. Your mind was open; you didn't close communication. But not really, it was just a routine kind of acceptance. It was his job not to slam the door, not yet.

Renata was alone with the ghosts. She was more aggressive in her own defense, as she reported them and there was no official intervention. You have heard before that old counselor Soto and his son enacted a rape together on the first or second weekend of the year. Now that she seemed not to get any help, and besides, she was not even dejected, their revenge cutthroat action increased its vocabulary. While tracking her around the clock, her head would be tapped by the wirelike device, sometimes accompanied by leg pressure, by energy closing in on her thorax like two big hands, as if to measure it was her breathing and not someone else's, and bringing in the heaviest pressure from their den of torture to see if they could make her stop being---when she laid down to sleep, when she sat at the library reading, while at the grocery store. It was electronic stalking for life. It was a continuous waking her up, anytime, entering her house and making noises, like the night of February 15/16. The son went in and out around the window, like a playful child, waving his magic wand around Renata' house as expression of his powerful persona, triumphant, with a fairy tale costume---his signature ghost.

They acted as if they owned the city, and never ever would they have to answer to the Law for what they do to drive her out. And I am more committed than ever to justice, responsibility, and to Renata.

THIRTY-TWO

THE DISTINCTION OF FAMILIAR PLACES

Dropping by the Caribbean Community Center was not a casual event in Rafi's civilian life. There were all these memories stuck to the walls and things, like living cells pumping their breathing toward his presence, all that contradictory past, going back to where he belonged, a great longing for the smallest sign of certainty that he still counted here, where he had suffered.

He never knew what his mother felt when he accepted a job in the old hometown. She didn't answer his questions. Maybe she, like he himself, didn't know what the feeling was. Now Rafi respected her silence more than ever, her non-interference. Without knowing it, this answer/non-answer set him free.

His aim was to talk to Director López as a citizen, as a former member that he was of this center, about his mother. He wanted to get to know him better than one can know anyone in a professional context, just by expanding the possibilities of time together, by asking any question, by telling one's own stories.

Rafi was investigating the Baptist minister's death, yes, but he was even more curious about the rumor he had heard of a certain Soto being López's lover. This was his day off, and he could allow himself to express feelings he would have thought unworthy of Rafin Salcedo, the officer. He hoped with all his heart they were the same person, this Soto youngster. If this were the case, he was in luck.

López came down to the community meeting room and greeted Salcedo in a warm manner. Rafi's first thought was that López was hiding something; otherwise, the meeting would have taken place in the director's office. Meeting here around the big classroom table was a way of preventing any kind of intimacy, of depth.

"Mr. Salcedo, I understand your mother used to work here in this building."

"Yes. She was the best community outreach worker that I have known. Found quickly and all by herself the people who needed help the most. Quite a talent."

"You got your own talent from her then. I hear you are sort of a hero in these parts. The kind cop, they say."

"I have great admiration for my mother. I owe her a lot. Thank you."

There was a silence, in which López betrayed his uneasiness, very slightly, but enough for Rafi to understand the extent of the self-control of the man. Rafi decided to exploit this worry in a novel way for López, by attributing it to something harmless, such as lack of funds, and so forth.

"Tell me, is it hard to find adequate support for your programs? I would like to help."

The obvious relief that López manifested, even when trying hard to hide it, reassured Rafi that he was on the right track. Rafi told himself he was not deceiving the director; he really wanted to help. An investigative cop was always looking for information, and he himself was not an exception. And so he tried to gear the conversation toward education, specifically science.

"Funding is the golden child of community nonprofits, as you may guess. If we can build a good case around our necessities and our programs being worthier than others, more promising for the long-term relief of poverty and ignorance, making it clear that we make it possible for the less fortunate to prepare themselves to be productive members of society, the donations increase; yes, we do quite well then. Although it's a continuous struggle. We never have the option of getting too comfortable."

López was very careful with the language he chose for his formal presentation to Rafi, standard concepts used in grant-writing, probably all learned from copies of copies. Very correct. Rafi smiled and leant back on the metallic folding chair where he was seated, around the long table.

"Well, with the increase in the number of nonprofits come advantages and challenges. There were no such problems when I was a child. This place was it. But convincing the system that we were part of society, and that changes had to be made for us to participate in the distribution of wealth was not easy. The only thing they understood was charity, not equality. You are benefitting from our work."

"We know, Mr. Salcedo! And we are grateful. Say, some day we should talk about the possibility of naming our ESL classroom after your mother."

"That's a great idea! She would be so proud! But tell me, do you have classrooms for all subjects, such as science?"

López did miss a beat but recovered almost as if nothing had happened. This man, the cop-turned-neighborhood Latino overnight, was a thorn on his chest. What did he want? He was not poor nor uneducated, and in that sense, he didn't belong there. López didn't need his money. His presence was not welcome. And even as he was thinking all this, López must smile.

"Yes, there is a computer room and an intelligent board, very useful nowadays. The kids expect you to be modern."

"Ah, yes. I've seen it."

There was an uncomfortable silence. Rafi calculated being careful. He was on the right road. The other man continued, smiling with his mouth only, but stiff and guarded like a guilty corpse awaiting his sentence.

"Do not hesitate to ask about tours or demonstrations. Our tutors are at your service."

Rafi saw his big chance. Must take it. He could not let it pass, come what may. Going directly to the heart of the matter was the best, the only one that could save him from López's suspicion, even if that's what would happen--- that the director suspected something. But he was not hiding anything. The question, or one facet of the question, was in full view.

"Is a young man named Soto one of your science tutors?"

López stood up quickly and checked his phone. "Please forgive me. I forgot I must make a phone call at this time." He walked to the door and turned his head only to say, summoning help from all his muscles so as not to completely betray himself: "I will check the names of all the tutors and get back to you."

Rafi said goodbye with his right hand from the chair where Director López had invited him to sit. He didn't envy López, although the man had great self-control. It would be much needed in the days to come. Rafi was to start right away to prepare an accusation of murder against Ferdinand Soto Jr., basing it on the corpse's description and the possible causes stated by the forensic investigation.

But what had given Rafi the needed information was Renata's description of the abuse, the same actions, the same perfect crime.

THIRTY-THREE

UNEXPLORED FIELDS OF LOVE

She would explain it someday. Well, not explain, but tell she should. Now, as soon as that now could be.

Unbelievable as it was, Renata's daring had given the universe an idea for some kind of resolution. For Renata's dignity, she could start telling this way--- as an introduction to a confession to Rafi. She was ready.

The problem was whether he would believe her. She couldn't do anything about that part. Her business was truth. And she started reviewing in her mind how the Pauli Ghost story happened, but not the part about the figure of a man who visited her once, hovering over her bed for ten seconds, like in the Cocteau movie, when the poet dreamt that his death visited him.

Renata's story was deeper. No one believed there was a ghost, which meant she was alone treasuring her memories. Everybody knew death, whether as beautiful as the poet saw her or as a toothless, old, greedy woman. Renata had to deal with the tragedy, beautiful in its own terrible way, alone.

Not even her ghost pitied her. But there was some similitude. The poet was in love with his death. And Renata was attached to her friendly ghost, to the memory.

She had accepted the Pauli visits, observing, but she was won over by the warmth and gentleness of her ghost. She didn't ask herself openly who Pauli was. But she knew, she guessed. The magic didn't inspire the rational, only the playful and the accepting.

One day, she told him she loved him. She did that twice. She told the ghost, as he was loving her, that she also felt love for him. Could she see him in the body to reciprocate his caresses?

Renata could sense his amazement, his not knowing what to do. He stopped. He retreated. He came back. He said nothing.

One night, there were random noises in Renata's room. Pauli the Ghost didn't come to the lovers' meeting. Instead, the noises sounded like someone tripping over an object, bumping against the wall. At some point, Renata thought the man who was Pauli could be doing drugs. Pauli was beautiful. But the time spent with computers and experiments designing this beauty could have warped him as a human being. Approaching someone's soul with gentleness, and then destroying that harmony with dissonance and randomness, was the beginning of Hubber's descent into the danger zone that Renata had tried to warn him about.

Probably the man had to engage in that destruction to go back to some state of mind demanded by his own lack of clarity in relationships, especially with those who didn't fit into the new order of the street where he had bought his first home, where he was lonely.

The morning after the night when Pauli the Ghost had not been present, Renata heard muffled tones of giggling. The rude woman of the quantum experiments was there. Pauli the Ghost had died, somehow opening the door to the Soto's brutality, as if love did not have a future where there is no equality or responsibility for the other.

Yes, this would be a good way to start telling Rafi about Pauli.

THIRTY-FOUR

A FORMER GIRLFRIEND

Rafi left alone the community center, after the sudden and unceremonious departure of the director.

"Sudden, but not unexpected," said Rafi aloud to himself.

Going down the street to the W. Meredith Poets Café for takeout food to sustain him in the long afternoon that awaited him while designing Torres' killer documents, he heard his name called from the other side. He saw a woman's arms waving, as if to help her thin voice with communication.

"Rafi, is that you?"

That voice, that body of long ago, was coming to him in happiness now! It was wonderful, but it couldn't be true. But it was---Fina, his first love. They had met when they were still children, and then each one took their own road, which seemed then so different! They were growing, each with interests and dynamics of their own. Rafi had thought she was angry at him when the relationship was over, that breaking up was his fault. But here she was now, smiling at him, calling his name. He smiled and waved. They were ready for the reconciliation.

"Fina! Wait, I'll cross." He jumped across the street to hug Fina, the same smiling, slim Fina of his memory.

They didn't say anything for a while, holding hands, a bit teary, with the happiness brought about by the release of a sorrow of youth.

"I saw you coming out of the center."

"Yeah, just met with the director. But tell me, where have you been?"

Fina put her hand on Rafi's arm softly, leading him away from the community center building, toward the coffee shop. "I try to stay away from the center. Are you going to get involved there?"

Rafi didn't answer at once, trying to understand the meaning of what his friend was saying. They walked together into the Poets' Café, and they ordered coffee and brought a menu to the little table by the window.

"You know I am a policeman, don't you?"

"Yes."

"Well, how can I start explaining this? Why are you staying away from the place?"

"Because I am a board member. The last one, the only one. López refuses to accept my resignation."

"Wait a minute! That's messed up! Why would he want to do this?"

"We have been noticing things that have made the board very uncomfortable: funds missing, evasive answers, promising expense reports that never came, and people dropped out, not wanting to be responsible for irregularities we didn't authorize. I am the only Latina and the only one truly connected to the center. All the others are not from here, so they disconnect easily. López says I must stay so he can say he has a board and do his things."

"Yeah, it makes sense," Rafi mumbled to himself.

Fina was looking at him, waiting for an answer. It didn't make sense to her.

"I know it doesn't make sense to you. But I hope to prove it does soon."

"Torres's death?"

"Yes."

"Do you think it is related? They say he died of a heart attack."

"Yes, I know. And I can't say anymore. Only this. Don't go in there. If you feel uncomfortable about anything, call me."

They talked about jobs, families, marriages, and people they knew in high school, until Rafi's food was ready. They left together for her car, and Rafi decided to take a walking detour when he saw the young Latino man, with a hood and a mustache, standing across from the Poet's Café, then following them. It was Soto's strategy. The same man, or a colleague, had stalked Renata.

Rafi spread a big sheet of paper on his all-purpose table and drew the basement space where the Baptist minister, Torres, died: the distance from the computer room, his closeness to the big trash can, and the plastic cleaning pails. Although Torres had been working on the computer he always used and his briefcase was with him, there was no trace of papers on the counter.

However, just to help himself think out different possibilities, Rafi drew a piece of paper on the counter where the computer was, turned on. He sketched a light here or a shadow there to imagine how it could have been at the moment of truth, which is the moment of peril. He had seen the photos taken of the body: the eyes wide open in terror, one hand outstretched toward the trash can and another on his crotch, as if protecting it, and his shirt open. And there were no marks on the skin, no bruises, no scratches, no blood, but Torres was a dead man.

Renata's words came to him with a deeper meaning. "If I were to fall down the stairs as they push me with their invisible hands, or if my heart could not take the upset, the fright, of their accosting me the whole night long, nobody would know what had happened because there are no marks. No signs. No digital prints. It's the perfect crime."

The perfect crime. Why? If there were no papers, why would the Baptist minister have an open briefcase? Why would he be near a turned-off computer? Why was he, in the evening, in the computer room his church shared with the community center? Who knew he was there? Not his family. They thought he was at the church preparing the service for Sunday. He had a key for the basement door. Of course, security cameras would know. But then, this crime was an inside job, if you knew so much about the minister's whereabouts.

Of course, all these questions were relevant if you think it wasn't a natural heart attack. There was such an implication of violence. Although beyond the wild, terrified eyes and the half-opened shirt, there were no scratches, no blood, or no signs of weapons.

Rafi thought of the suffering that the position of the body suggested, protecting his genitals, like Renata had to do. He saw the half-unbuttoned shirt, as if he had been taunted by a hand that was not a hand. It left no marks but slashed the chest with a powerful energy intent on domination, even annihilation, the harsh pushing around, the fight for the control of something important, such as that paper he had drawn at the start, as necessary for the contentious scenario.

What would that paper, if it existed, say? Why would the minister have it there in that basement? Was he having a meeting with anyone? Informal opinions gathered around town painted the dead man as kind and very honest. He never mistrusted anyone, even if he had a reason. One possibility, thought Rafi, could be that he scheduled a meeting with López to talk about missing funds, if there were any accounts or funding that they shared.

Rafi made a list of questions and requests for investigators. One of the requests was to check the Baptist minister's phone records, in case he talked with López the day of his death. Rafi had come to a conclusion, and now his interest was concentrated on detecting where Soto Jr. had made a mistake. He was the brain and the executor, almost without a doubt. López was merely the remote sex partner facilitating the acquisition of a big chunk of money, which would be disappearing soon, leaving no trace behind. This question about the shared funding was one that Rafi must keep secret from López and Soto Jr. They must not suspect that he knew.

That's where his former girlfriend, Fina, could really help. His only qualm was that it could put her in danger. However, she already had been singled out as the one board member who was still there but not cooperating.

The first thing Rafi did was to text his former girlfriend from a police phone number that, if traced, gave a phony name in the area, with voice mail to leave a message. The instructions were not to call him at his personal number. She would be given one of these phony numbers and only for texting him. He was (almost) sure that Ferdinand Soto Jr. had her number bugged.

THIRTY-FIVE

THE CRIMINAL LIFE

"Wait! Wait! Wait! I need to get this right. You mean you showed up in court and waited all day until two in the afternoon. The prosecutor called, you went in front of the judge, and they told you they pass. Is that what you said?"

"Yes. At first, I didn't move. The judge looked at me as if not believing it and said again, 'We pass.' I said, 'Thank you,' and left."

"Any ideas?"

"Yes. One of them. The document didn't accuse me of anything---there were just some mental health notes that Soto Jr, the invisible lover, placed there, as if from the police, and that invoice for cleaning his car, an eight-hundred-dollar job. I had told the prosecutor I wanted to see that because that's not why I was arrested."

"She didn't show you."

"No. She said something about an attorney walking me through it."

Rafi touched Renata's hand and smiled. Things were beginning to happen, and that was a good sign. The long wait had been the hardest for his friend, that eternity of evil, the greed for its accumulating merits, as if it would never be enough.

"But you do not qualify for a public defender, right?"

"No. I'm too rich. If there is one thing that puts your life in perspective, it is being in one of those courtrooms. Your rights being read in public, the auditorium full like a free theater, and onlookers waiting for you to show more sins than they have, gloating if you fall. The poverty. The lack of hope. I had the feeling that Soto was there, hiding in the back in the shadows, ogling me and licking his chops with pleasure at my public exposure, plus pocketing all that money. At least the red van and I returned home at the same time. Someone had been there. I saw a whole bunch of kids that looked like the gang members who had been stalking me. Right away, the picking at my head with the electric wires started. They knew I had not paid again. The torture would be ferocious that night, and all the nights that followed. And one more chapter of vandalizing my car."

"So how do you think it happened?"

"A gift from Unk's ... You smile, but how else do you explain it?"

"A miracle."

"Or an example of causality. Unk had a profound effect on his students, whether they liked him or not. He was a powerful figure in their lives. And here I am, representing him somehow, suffering an injustice, the way he also suffered injustices, with integrity. I greeted this guy, an attorney whom I knew had been his student. He remembered me walking with Unk to the river every Sunday morning. I could see him sitting back down after representing his clients, looking at me sideways all the time I was in the courtroom, maybe determining whether I was guilty; then maybe he went to the prosecutor's, looked at my folder and made a decision. Risky for him, but not really. He could always say I am innocent, from a good family in town. So, I believe he recommended they throw it out. And when the public defender looked for him, he was gone."

"Delightful, if it happened that way."

"It could have happened that way, so let's enjoy the story. An example of lateral thinking: you wouldn't expect it."

"And that day? With the Sotos?"

"Ghetto stuff. They started trying to burn the skull once more, followed by unbearable pressure around the ribs. But I moved, stood up, went to another room, and tapped arms and chest. And I cursed and cursed, awful language I produced. They gave up for a while. Someone, Soto Jr., the lover, came around the house around two in the morning and spoke something darkly toward my window. Fear tactics are all they have.

"Then I woke up around four. They were attacking my legs, touching and trying to reach my crotch. I defended myself the best I could, half-asleep. Then they vandalized my car again a few days later, the same people, the same pattern on the hood. The court thing was a miracle. When will it come, the next much needed one?"

"Ask the universe. Your turn now."

"Do you believe what you're saying, Rafi?'

"Logic tells me no. But I'm a believer."

Renata thought about Rafi's answer. Coming from anybody else, it would have sounded commonplace, empty. But he was right. She had to believe that someone would, out of duty or compassion, step forward with an answer; someone who was not afraid of the gang, as Dup had been, calculating risks; or someone, the scientist who teaches particle physics and could arrive at the conclusion that this was an excellent real-life specimen of Schrödinger's fear of quantum phenomena in the everyday world, showing that science and math represented something beyond pretty designs on the blackboard.

Someone, an assistant judicial member of the River Guard Institute reading Renata's letter asking for help and clarification of the science behind the dark abusers, decided to go the justice way rather than the tribal one chosen by the local police.

Rafi looked at Renata thoughtfully. The woman had a heart. She had suffered this long indignity, and she didn't have a bad word for anyone. She lived with the unshakable hope that her street, which stood for all the other streets in the world, could be free from terror, simply a path to peace.

None of them expected the note that came in the mail in a few days, calling Renata back to court, without an explanation, as usual.

Renata texted Hubber, asking for his assistance. There was silence, as usual. She knew something of Hubber, communicated to her through Pauli---a gentleness that could be revealed only in the dark, without a body to be made responsible for it, a yearning for a love that, if he had made a decision to follow his heart, would compromise him with the environment that had accepted him solely on the basis of his rejection of Renata.

What to do with the love that Pauli had shown her? Was that all in the past? If all he could do was keep silent, what was his spirit saying? What was he afraid of? What kept him withdrawn from this clear bid for peace?

THIRTY-SIX

A WEB OF BUGS

The days following Rafi's visit to Director López were days of tranquility around the Caribbean Community Center. López was there, taking calls and answering messages and making plans for writing grants and creating programs, such as the projected block party for the summer. He was especially proud of this

"The neighborhood hasn't had its joint celebration in how long? Four years? That's too long, man!"

And often, without a specific reason, or to anybody, he added:

"We need to bring back the community spirit. The community is our backbone."

He went on like this, community this and community that, although he didn't live around here. *Community* was a key concept in grant writing, like *underserved communities*. "The cities are for the poor," he said to others like him at conventions, "unless you own a mansion by the river". But he boasted of his private apartment in the woods, gated with guard, without snooping neighbors. Life was conducted through surveillance cameras, phones you didn't have to answer, and managing companies. And the best thing: his current wife paid for it.

He did not forget to send Rafi the list of tutors. After consulting with his lover, Soto Jr. was included on the list as a bilingual volunteer for wireless systems.

"Like for fucking in the shower virtually," Soto added this in his low *Ohhh-Ahhh* sensual gangway of using anyone for his pleasure, especially if Soto Jr. used force. He liked it this way best.

They both laughed. They got together all the time now since Ferdinand had learned the ghost way from his family. There were so many delicious ways of using it, like visiting his lover López at dawn and doing it right there, with the wife asleep nearby, or in the office's bathroom, or in the office, period. López locked the door and busied himself with the computer while Ferdinand caressed him.

Rafi had thanked López for the list. All the tutors seemed to be well-behaved individuals working for established institutions. They would be contacted if there were any questions, Rafi had added, but he didn't think there would be any need. All was in order.

The lovers celebrated. They should let time pass, help choose a new Baptist minister, be good neighbors, and celebrate often, as often as Director López was available through their remote connection.

"One day soon we'll have all the time in the world." This is what López had said to Ferdinand, Dina, in a bout of passion.

He dreamt of grabbing the man himself, not this empty space that the virtual ghost offered. He himself was touched and caressed, López had said. But his own hands were empty. And he wanted to change that. Ferdinand, Dina, smiled, sounding out his *Ahhh-Ohhhh* signature pleasure sound. But he didn't think so. López would not be invited to the big party when he, Dina, became rich.

Through board records that Fina made available, Rafi located a funding source, a private donor with a large estate who had transferred $2 million for a joint Caribbean chapel. This could be at the heart of the story, and the question, for Rafi, was how to know whether the money was in the lovers' hands, without raising suspicion that would jeopardize finding the killer. Fina would not know. But records from the Baptist minister's phone showed messages between the two men the day the pastor died. Rafi was interested in a call López made to the minister around eight thirty. The time of death was calculated around eight seventeen that evening. And the text messages read that the two had scheduled a meeting at seven forty-five.

Rafi had not decided yet how to approach López regarding those calls. He would, after investigating Soto a bit more. There was some dynamic he didn't want to interfere with, when Renata called him from her home landline, avoiding the cell phone altogether, which the Sotos bugged. Lover was putting big traveling bags into his car, she informed. Earlier, the bank had notified him that one of the Caribbean Center accounts, recently moved into the folder named Building Community, had been transferred to an Alternative Investment Fund that was already in place, with the director as the sole signatory. The time was now.

Rafi, in civilian clothes and driving a brown car, activated the alarms with town and state police. But he had a hunch: the white sports car would not leave town. He made a desperate call to Renata, her home line.

"What's the name of the garage in the invoice?"

"Silvia's Body Shop."

And that's where invisible lover was found, inside the garage, all doors down and locked, his bags already inside a nondescript gray car with dark windows. The expensive white car, without a license plate, was being turned into an elegant black specimen.

Director López got into the police car, without questioning anything, without trying to defend himself. A finished man, but with that last shred of dignity of those who are not evil and are secretly glad their association with wrong is over.

Rafi looked at him, and López lowered his eyes, accepting the moral superiority of the man he had left alone in the big downstairs room just a few days before. If he'd had that day the strength to say, "This is what's happening. I am guilty, yes, but not that guilty. I can prevent those funds from disappearing."

But, Salcedo thought, *López doesn't have in his life the women that he, Rafi, had been blessed with*. And that made all the difference. He thought of his mother, the woman with the accent who was made ashamed of herself because of it, but now would have a room bearing her name in the community center. He would see to it that López's idea became reality.

And he thought of Fina, the childhood friend who awakened love inside his clumsy adolescent breast first, with a sweet smile born for welcoming him into the universe of a higher form of friendship and feeling. But things interfered in that path, distractions, petty ambitions, and the ideas that the system pour into your consciousness. There was more to achieve, more to learn, farther to go. How was it that he and Fina grew apart? But they had not really been torn apart. It was an interlude. She welcomed him back with the same light with which she loved him then, and he was ready for the moment of forgiveness.

And Abuela, gracias, abuela! From you, I learned to dream with my eyes open. And Renata, Nata, the cream of his present, the gentle woman branded a criminal by this corrupt system of ours, stood strong and unwavering in her quest to get to the truth. She was the true hero in this story---she and Fina together. They both gave him essential insights into the almost-perfect crime that Soto Jr., the promising future politician, had envisioned in order to betray all in sight, including López, whom he mocked with false love. It was an almost-perfect crime to swindle his very own community, which he pretended to want to serve in the future as a public servant.

The idea of community must be brought here prominently, the day he made his public presentation and referred to López's message. It was that he had been sidetracked, López had been. But we should give all of us an opportunity and learn from this terrible chapter written in the Book of Chance and Fate.

THIRTY-SEVEN

WAVES

Rafi chose the new meeting place. It had always been this way, but Renata sensed that now their world was essentially different, and he meant to underline that change in their spiritual status by taking her to those magical places of his imagination that had always been there, but with no one to share them with, and sort of abandoned. They had come together at a period of distress---their stormy present, a point of realignment, of defining their response to the world.

So, it was not enough to have tea at Manny's today. There was a clear landscape opening to their lives that needed a scenario more appropriate for the freedom they had earned. It had nothing to do with big houses, chairs, or vacations, but with a new way of walking in the world.

He suggested the beach, a gathering midmorning by the rocks, at the cove, the special spot already taking root in their memory as the "one": cradled by the singing of the waves, at ease with space and the rhythm of time.

Coming down into the boardwalk from the back entrance, Renata saw Rafi standing on the rocks that had grown away from the land into the sea space, like an arm stretched out to the unknown, trusting they had a future. There was nobody else around, and yet all was complete. Without him, there would have been only desolation.

When choosing the beach over the boardwalk to reach him, Renata was showing her delight at being there. Rafi saw her coming and moved his body toward her. He glanced at himself, too. The white shirt open at the collar and a new gray wool sweater, soft to the touch, was very important to exorcise the memory of the coarse brown of his early youth, and the warm light gray corduroys. Thinking about his looks had been an attitude he did not wish to cultivate; maybe he was too attracted to the idea in a narcissistic manner. But now he was serious. It was important. He wanted to support Renata in all aspects of life. His persona was as relevant as other valuables.

This was another consideration, valuables and values. He thought he knew Renata so well by now, but he should not ever think that way. To love somebody, he was sure, meant setting the person free. And to think that one knew the other's thoughts, somehow, was limiting their rights to grow, to change. But he understood what he meant, yes. He was sure of her integrity, more than of anything. It was a feeling, a reminder to engage the heart always.

"We got lucky! What great weather!"

Rafi got down from the rocks to greet her. "Yes. I checked all the weather channels in sight before choosing the beach! And they sent us the best weather."

"You seemed so thoughtful up there! I kept looking at you and thinking I should go around and take a long time to get there. He's seeing something beautiful, I thought."

"I was seeing you, yes!"

They laughed. Renata looked at the shells on the sand and picked a few. Rafi considered the inadequacy of the shoes they were wearing to cross to the other side of the cove and decided against it. It was high tide.

"We'll do it this summer! That's something I always wanted to do."

"How did you know I was considering jumping to the other side?"

"I heard you thinking!"

"No! You read my mind! I must be careful now with what I think!"

"You should always be careful what you think anyways." Renata liked Rafi's humor. It left open the possibility of entering into a serious exchange of points of view.

"Always right. Yes, that is true. Why is it true? Because we don't want others to know we are not really that trustworthy …"

"No. Unk used to say that our thoughts are our guides. To make the right decisions, one should be well-guided."

Rafi thought about Renata's wisdom for a while, looking at the rhythmic movement of the waters. Renata busied herself with the stones and shells and smiled at Rafi's response.

"I like what you say. And not because it comes from Unk."

"No? Aren't you trying to flatter me?"

"Certainly not. If I were trying to do that, I would not be here today."

"Great answer! It's the same for me. My private time is the most valuable, always unpaid."

"Not just anybody can be part of that … how would I call it … space/time/magic dream state. It's not even the kind of time we measure in hours and minutes. It's something else. It is infinity achieved in mortal life. It is happiness tasted, a glimpse of the soul … There exists nothing tangible at that point, just … just …”

And Rafi smiled, not bothering to add more words because he was holding Renata's hand and they were walking very close to the waves, listening.

New London, Connecticut
August 12, 2024